NORTHERN LIGHTS

BOYD CRAVEN

Northern Lights
By Boyd Craven

Many thanks to friends and family for keeping me writing!

To be alerted of new releases, please sign up for my mailing list here:
http://eepurl.com/bghQb1

TABLE OF CONTENTS

CHAPTER 1

It's all about the weight. That, and the fact that I am the heaviest in our group. I know, that doesn't make a lot of sense, but when you are hiring a float plane to fly some friends to a remote hunting and fishing camp, I guess it makes sense. Weight means the pilot has to burn more fuel, too much weight means all kinds of nefarious things when it isn't handled properly, according to my pilot, Bill. Everything from takeoff and landing distances, to going through too much fuel too fast, running out and crashing. We don't want to crash so we were mindful… And weighed in with our gear.

Tracy and Brian were the first two to make the trip to Pringle Lake, in the Northern Territories of Canada. They had their packs and rods. That was it. The bush pilot plus them and their packs weighed enough that he could make the trip and have about an hour's worth of fuel remaining when he landed. The three-and-a-half-hour round trip was done, and the pilot refueled while Jordan loaded his gear and the food. We had enough dried goods to last us the two weeks we'd be down there... But weight restrictions.

When Bill made it back it was my turn. I'd already weighed in earlier in the day, and everyone had had a laugh at my expense. I'd done my calculations and I'd come in gear plus my body weight at exactly the 350-pound limit. Jordan had been exceptionally biting in his remarks about me packing down to the last pound, but that's what a good prepper does. Since we were heading into the northern territories, I wanted to be ready for anything.

"Hey Tom, you never told me why you've got half your stuff in buckets," Bill said, passing me on the dock so he could start the refueling process.

"Got some gear packed into them," I told him.

"They make good camp stools, when you're sitting outside by the fire pit," he said grinning.

"They do." I could just as easily have stacked them into one, nesting them in layers, but the four buckets I had packed contained a small supply of food plus my camping/fishing gear.

One of them also held my camp gun, a .22 that folded up into its stock, and about 500 rounds of ammunition. Since I was about 230lbs and a tad overweight, I had about 120lbs that I could take in with me. The first thing I weighed at home was a case of Miller, and then figured there wouldn't be enough for the 2-week trip without having Bill fly us more out the first week, so a few pounds went into three bubble wrapped bottles of Jack Daniels.

I might be roughing it, but there was no point pretending I wasn't going to have a good time. The other gear I packed was just as vital and potentially life-saving. See, I'd gotten into prepping when I was a young kid. I'd loved to trap, hunt, and fish from a young age. I'd grown up in a sleepy little town near Argentine, Michigan, and I spent many an afternoon at the back of the property, trying to figure out the wildlife, making forts, or camping.

We didn't own a lot of land, but it was wild land, untamed, and my little sister used to joke that we called it the 'underworld' because it was where no other men had trodden. I did though, and I used to make little first aid kits, and then a fire-starting kit... then I learned how to snare animals; pests at first and then rabbits, squirrels and even birds. Soon a snare kit went into my kits... and it started being half a backpack full. These days my kit consists of a few buckets and a backpack for the basics I expect I'll need for two weeks.

A heavy Coleman sleeping bag, a pillow... both of which have been shrunk in size by a glad vacuum seal bag, food, snares, my gun, various knives, a camp hatchet, machete, tackle, bug spray, and three rods. I did remember to bring clothes but I will admit, they were almost an afterthought as was the lightweight spring jacket. That had been the biggest point of Jordan's ribbing. It was summer time and I was packing a jacket.

BOYD CRAVEN

Didn't it get cold heading up towards the North Pole? Besides, it was the only waterproof coat I had and I don't like the plastic ponchos that don't breathe. When they asked what was in the buckets and if I could take some of their gear since I was flying last, I got on the scale with all of my stuff and told them sorry, but no. I'd literally taken over two weeks to weigh, pack, and get everything perfect. I even cut 2lbs of body weight by fasting so I could have the room needed for an emergency radio. It might seem a little weird, but they were my quirks, and being single I didn't see any reason to change my weirdness to please somebody else.

"Once I fuel her up, I'm going to head to the bathroom. You need to go before we take off?" Bill asked me.

"No sir, went right before you landed. Truth be told, I might crawl in and take a nap if you don't mind?"

"Not at all," he said and finished off the fueling and headed into the little building at the end of the large gravel parking lot.

I'd spent quite a bit of time in that building, watching old sitcom reruns like Cheers and Seinfeld while I waited for my turn. I was bored to tears waiting, but I couldn't sleep. The receptionist was constantly on the phone with who I could only assume to be her husband or boyfriend, talking nonstop. That wouldn't normally bug me, except as soon as I settled into a comfortable spot, the phone would ring again, somebody would pull up enquiring about a flight, or someone would start arguing about the weight limit restrictions.

Honestly, I knew ahead of time that their Otter was down and we were going in the smaller Cessna, so I had planned for it. The Otter would have cut the trip from 3 flights down to 1 or 2, but the outfitter didn't charge us extra for that. In fact, they apologized profusely and told us that the part had to be ordered in because the airframe they used was from the 70s and they don't make them like they used to... Great... Old and hard to find parts for...

I finished stashing my buckets, fishing rods and tackle box, and put my backpack behind the seat. I had room to spare if I could grease my way into the seat. The Cessna wasn't meant for guys my size. Not that I was a big weight lifter, quite the opposite in fact, I could probably stand to lose twenty or thirty pounds, and that was something I was hoping to get a jumpstart on during this trip. Once I was wedged into my seat I sat back.

The waves on the plane's pontoons were soothing as the plane rocked back and forth. I was starting to drift off when the door opened and Bill was standing there, holding out two Styrofoam cups. I took them and he got in and buckled up. He took one of the cups back and tilted it, and I bumped cups with him like two dudes clinking beer bottles together.

"Just because you're roughing it doesn't mean you have to live your life without coffee," he grinned.

"Thanks. How long is the flight going to be?" I asked.

"Oh, about an hour and a half for you if the

wind is at our backs like it was last trip. Three and a half to four hours overall for me."

I eyeballed the coffee cup and raised my eyebrows at him questioningly.

"Hey, y'all have an outhouse there, and it's my last flight of the day."

"Yeah, just messing with you," I told him.

Bill was older than me by at least twenty years, but it was hard to say exactly. His skin was tanned in a way that only comes from being outdoors all times of the year, and to be honest, this farther north and the UV rays were stronger than they were even thirteen hours south to where I was. He had crowfeet around his eyes and his hair and mustache were salt and pepper black on white. He wasn't one of those guys who killed you in a handshake, nor was he overly competitive, but he was quiet and comfortable with silence.

"That's no problem. So, you excited to get this show on the road?" he asked, checking off something on his clipboard and then flipping a few toggles.

"Yeah! Ready when you are."

Takeoff was more fun than anything else you could do with your clothes on. It was nothing like a takeoff in a jet. At first, the waves on the lake bumped against the pontoons shaking things and giving me a minute's worry, but it smoothed out as the plane gained speed and my stomach almost fell out as he pulled back on the stick and we took to the air gently. It was loud, but only about half as loud as the time I flew to Disney with an ex of mine.

Bill motioned for me to put on a pair of headphones and I did, adjusting the microphone so it wasn't mashed against my lips.

"I'll be able to hear ya with this on. Now, you have any questions about the trip?"

I'd researched them thoroughly, read everything on their website, looked at every picture and followed every blog that mentioned them.

"How good is the fishing?" Lame, I know, I asked it.

"You'll be sick of catching fish tomorrow," Bill told me.

"Really?" I asked, surprised.

"Really," he said, putting the plane into a slow turn, "There's so much walleye and northern pike in that lake. Nobody fishes it but us."

"You mean the company?" I asked.

"No, guys like you and your friends. There's only one cabin on the lake you know?"

I didn't apparently. "No, I didn't," I told him, "So when we get sick of fishing, what do you recommend?" I asked him.

"Drinking games," he said, a real talker.

"That's not going to be fun with only one girl there," I grumbled.

"Yeah, that's going to make things interesting for sure. Even a week alone up here with someone else's lady... I've seen it strain friendships. That's why with a 2-week trip like you guys are taking, I'll still be flying out in a few days to check in on you, and again next week and then the pickup."

"Wait, you've had guys fight over somebody else's wife?" I asked, curious now despite myself.

Not that I was interested in Tracy; I actually despised the woman and had almost cancelled out of my trip when Brian insisted she come. It was Jordan who'd convinced me to stick with it.

"Oh yeah, fist fights, and one time a guy even cut his other friend. That's one more thing, I'm sure it's been hammered home to ya, but I gotta say it again, don't get hurt. Don't do something stupid… because a few days seems like a short amount of time, but it's not. Not if you flip your boat, break a leg or need stitches."

"I'll try to remember that," I said, "I got some first aid stuff in my kit back there, just in case."

"Good, there's supplies in the cabin, but they are the basics. Gauze, Band-Aids, stinger extractors. I keep telling the boss to get us a little more supplies but he won't."

"Worried about liability?" I asked, even though I was probably the only one of the group who'd actually read the waiver we all had to sign before coming on this trip.

"Yeah, don't want some drunken hillbilly trying to stich himself up or kill himself 'cuz he watched one too many episodes of House or General Hospital."

"Yeah, I can see that," I admitted. "What about hunting?" I asked.

"Upland birds, rabbits, and squirrels I imagine

are good. Bears are active, so keep all your food locked up in the bear proof steel box and keep your garbage burned or buried. Moose have calves now… so stay away from any, otherwise they might stomp a mud hole in your ass."

"So plenty of wildlife?" I asked him.

"Yeah, it's one of the most beautiful places I've ever been."

I nodded and turned towards him. "You mind if I take a quick nap?"

"And miss out on all of this?" he chuckled, "Go ahead. I'm sure tonight there's going to be plenty of drinking and campfires. Get your rest in."

I was exhausted. I'd driven straight through for almost thirteen hours and waited another eight for the flight. It wasn't long before I put the microphone up away from my mouth and leaned my head back. The constant sound and thrumming sensation of the motor soon had me out cold.

CHAPTER 2

We're about to taxi in," Bill's voice startled me awake.

I sat up and rubbed my eyes, knocking the headphones loose a little bit. I fixed that and looked out the window as we were starting to descend. Everywhere I could see, lakes and rivers cut through an impressive amount of green treetops. We were still high up, but it was obvious to me that we were descending rapidly.

"How do you know which one? GPS?" I asked and Bill shook his head and pointed to his headphone.

It took me a minute to remember to put the microphone down near my mouth and I repeated my question, pointing to all the water.

"I've made this flight so many times I can do it

without my instruments. We've got cabins on about half the big lakes we passed on the way up here, so you get used to it, just like driving a car."

"That makes sense. Did we make good time?"

"About what I thought. You got about a good hour of sleep in, but I figured you'd like to be awake for the landing so I don't startle you."

"You're right," I admitted, "Thanks."

The lakes grew larger and larger as we descended until it was obvious which one we were going to be landing on. At the northwestern edge of the lake, I could make out a small clearing in the trees and the blocky shape of a cabin. A long dock stretched far out into the lake and I could make out the two aluminum boats tied off on one side of it.

"Looks like they're waiting for you," Bill said and I squinted.

On the dock, three figures stood and waved. I almost waved back and then realized that there'd be no way they'd see me. Instead, I waited. The landing was as gentle as the takeoff, and by that I mean it was rough at first and then smoothed out. The plane rocked side to side as our wake caught up to us and Bill let it come almost to a stop before taxiing up to the dock. I opened the door and hopped onto the dock and threw the heavy rope I found there across the piton on the pontoon.

"I got that," Bill said, "Get your gear, then I'm going to borrow your outhouse. Coffee." He explained.

"Ok. Hey, guys!" I said turning to greet everyone.

"Hey, hey," Brian said, holding his hand out.

The handshake turned into a hug and Jordan was next, a cold Budweiser can offered up in his free hand. What a friend! I took it and then hugged him too.

"You two get any fishing in yet?" I asked, watching as Bill finished tying off the boat.

"Limited out," Brian said sheepishly.

"All of you?" I asked.

"Yeah," Tracy said, "of walleyes at least. I've got some ready to go into the frying pan. Mr. Bill, you staying for dinner?"

Bill hesitated and then looked at me. I shrugged. Personally, I think her cooking tastes like death, but I wasn't about to be a critic. I had cans of spam in one of the buckets just in case.

"Sure, I'll stay for a piece of fish or so," he said after a minute and then handed me gear.

No shaking hands or hugs for Tracy. I tolerated her, berated her in my mind, though never in public, much.

The buckets were the easiest and Jordan took two of them right off the bat and walked into the cabin. I took my pack and two buckets, leaving Brian to grab a duffel bag with the coat and clothing. It clanked as the bug spray hit the can of Coleman fuel I had stashed between layers of sweaters. They must have worked themselves loose, but since I didn't smell anything they were merely noisy instead of leaking, which would have sucked.

"Come on in; me casa su casa," I motioned for Bill who seemed to be watching Tracy walking away slowly.

The view wasn't that great.

The death that was served to me on the plate wasn't horrible. In fact, it was pretty good.

"This is great," I told Tracy, "I didn't know you knew how to fry fish up like this."

"I looked it up before the trip. I figure that on my cooking days I can at least serve something edible."

"Not like that one time you burned the noodles cooking Easy Mac?" Jordan said and started giggling like a girl.

"You microwave Easy Mac, don't you?" Bill asked us.

I laughed at Tracy's horror-stricken face, and soon Brian was as well.

"Yes, but we're teaching her how to cook like a gourmet," Brian said, kissing her on the temple.

She calmed and took one last bite. It was good, I hadn't expected it, in fact, I was going to ask her later on what she'd used for the batter.

"Well, I have to get going," Bill said, "It'll be dark in another hour or two. Get a lot lighter up here," he said.

"Thanks for staying for dinner," Tracy said, the perfect hostess.

"Thank you, ma'am, that hit the spot. Hopefully, I won't fall asleep at the wheel," he said tipping an imaginary hat.

We all stood and followed him to the dock. He reassured us that he'd be out in four days to check on us and again early in the next week. We all said our goodbyes and watched as he fired up the plane and waited for it to warm up before he taxied away from the dock. The takeoff was just as graceful looking as it felt like when I rode with him, and soon he was soaring. He circled the lake briefly and, as the plane climbed, I realized that out here, there was no pollution and you could see forever.

"Looking for the northern lights?" Tracy asked me, bumping me with her hip.

"No," I said, "Just thinking how far you can see out here," I told her, annoyed with the contact.

Bill radioed in that he was heading back. He'd made the trip a thousand or more times. Other than reminding himself to pick up his medicine on the way home, it was the end of a nice day. He knew the last man he'd dropped off was partial to the other man's wife; he'd seen it and it worried him some. The only reason he mentioned it in the fly-in was that he'd noticed him eyeballing her before she'd left with Brian.

"Probably an old girlfriend," he muttered to himself, making the airplane climb.

As he started into the cloud layer, a flash of light had him squinting and then his radio went silent, the soft static no longer filling his ears, and then it hit him. He felt the pain in his chest immediately and he reached for the barf bag he kept for the passengers and puked. The crushing pain in his chest was horrible. After a moment's hesitation, and with one good arm, he turned the plane around slowly.

He rubbed at his chest; the scar from his pacemaker implant bugged him from time to time, but his chest felt hot, and the spot under the scar seemed to be the focal point of the pain. He threw up again and squinted through the worst of it. If he could get the plane landed again near the folks he just dropped off—

Bill slumped over, his body weight pushing the control stick of the plane just enough.

"He's turning around?" Tracy asked.

"Maybe he forgot something," Brian said kissing the top of her head.

"Maybe he's gotta use the john again," Jordan said and I grinned.

Tracy shot him an annoyed look and looked at me. Suddenly my face was stoic and I managed to avoid her seeing me share the grin.

"I don't know why he'd come back. The plane was pretty cleaned out when he dropped me off—"

"Oh, my God!" Tracy screamed.

I saw the airplane suddenly start to nose down, the right wing starting to dip.

"What's he doing?" Jordan asked, his voice matching the same worry I was feeling.

"He's going to crash," I said softly, praying I was

wrong.

There was literally nothing we could do but watch helplessly as the plane came in and hit the water half a mile from us, at about a twenty-degree angle. The nose hit first, followed by the right wing. The whole plane cartwheeled, sending up great geysers of water as parts of it literally disintegrated. We ran halfway back from the end of the dock, expecting to get hit with something, but by the time the water settled, the dock made it intact. The plane, not so much.

I jumped into the first aluminum boat that had a five horse pusher and pulled the ripcord. It smoked a bit but fired right up. Jordan and Brian jumped in with me without a word. Tracy just stood there on the dock, silent tears streaming down her face. Jordan threw off the line and I opened the throttle.

The plane was sinking, but how fast was hard to determine. Part of the fuselage was attached to enough of the airframe for the pontoons, but not by much. The other half had been torn away on impact. The front section where Bill sat was still above water, but only barely.

"Make it go faster," Brian screamed.

"It's already got the pedal to the metal," I screamed back.

We'd only been in the northern part of Canada for an hour and suddenly the motor and the wind seemed as loud as the crash of the plane. Luckily there was no fire. Within a minute, I was guiding the boat to the side of the plane and Jordan nearly leaped out of the boat and onto the leg of the pontoon. What was left of the fuselage was on its right side, the left-hand pilot's door out of the water by less than a foot.

"You stay with the boat," Brian instructed and I nodded. He jumped out of the boat into the water and swam up to the pontoon as Jordan opened the pilot's door.

His legs dangled in the air as he leaned in and I screamed in horror as the plane rolled under the waves. I'd let the boat idle but now I was moving it slowly closer to the bubbling area where it had been. The amazing thing was that the water was so clear, I could see straight down to the bottom, and it wasn't very deep. I could see my two friends struggling with a third figure, and I killed the motor in case they came up underneath me. I debated jumping in but suddenly Jordan pushed off the plane, surfaced then took a breath before diving again.

As if choreographed, Brian and Jordan grabbed Bill's coat and pushed off and started to swim up. I reached my arms down into the water as they broke the surface, grabbing Bill. Brian blew out his held breath and panted for a second as I tried to pull him in. I couldn't do it. He was too heavy for me to do it by myself without tipping the boat over.

"I need help," I said, gasping.

"Hold on," Jordan said, "I'll hop in from the back. Brian, hold onto the front. Tom, you keep hold of Bill."

"I got him," I said, and I grabbed Bill.

I felt the boat rock more than I was comfortable with. The back dipped and I saw that Jordan had levered himself into the back, and he crawled quickly up to the front left side as I held onto Bill's wet form. I couldn't tell if he was breathing, but I did keep his head out of the water.

"Ok, Brian, go to the other side and hold on so we don't tip the boat," he instructed.

I'm glad he was the one taking over because my mind had gone blank. Of everything I'd ever prepared for, I was drawing a blank and I was hating my inaction and lack of conscious thought.

"Ready," Brian called and together Jordan and I hauled Bill up by the arms.

"He's not breathing," I said checking.

The boat rocked again and Brian had pulled himself in the same way that Jordan had.

"Pulse?" he asked.

"Yeah, slow and thready," I told him, "And he's bleeding from a dozen places. I think his arm is broken," I said looking at the funny angle his hand was sticking out from his coat.

"Get us back to shore," Jordan said, "I'll do CPR."

Now I understood why Jordan didn't lock up like I did. As an EMT, he'd literally done this thousands of times. I quit kicking myself as Jordan and Brian started assessing Bill's injuries as I drove the damned boat back to the dock.

"Is he ok?" I asked them.

"He's breathing again," Jordan answered just as Bill turned his head and puked then took in a big deep breath.

The smell of lake water and coffee made me

feel sick to my stomach as well, but I didn't puke. I couldn't afford to. I'd thought of myself as the better-prepared guy on the trip, but what did I know? I could do barely more than play chauffeur here.

"Go in hot, Tracy will throw a line," Brian told me and I just nodded.

I left the throttle open, not caring about the wake, and cut it off as I got near the dock. A little 5 horse pusher can propel the boat to speeds upwards of a fast walk, but that was about it. I grabbed the line Tracy tossed to me and pulled the boat to a stop then tied it off as the other two picked up Bill and put him on the dock to check him over.

Bill groaned and retched again. One thing I'd missed in the crazy boat ride was the fact that they had pulled his shirt open. The area over his heart was discolored under a scar, and I wondered if that was from bruising from CPR.

"I didn't think you were supposed to move him?" I asked them, confused.

"We're alone out here," Tracy told me.

I just nodded and ran towards my buckets that had been left on the wooden deck of the cabin. I could at least bring the first aid supplies I'd packed away, even if I only knew how to use half of them. Jordan would know what everything was. I'd found a trauma kit from Emergency Essentials in a kid-sized backpack; I'd packed the rest of my first aid stuff in it, then wrapped it in a large 5 gallon Ziploc bag and sealed it.

I should buy stock in Ziploc, seriously.

"What you got?" Jordan asked as I was ripping

the lid off the bucket and pulling out the bag.

Brian was talking softly to Bill who was responding, his words so low I couldn't make them out.

"Trauma kit," I said ripping the bag open when I couldn't open it normally in my panic.

Jordan looked at me and nodded, giving me a wry smile. He'd always teased me about how overboard I go in prepping, how I should learn to use all the gear I buy and shelve as a just in case. Truth was, I do learn it but medical stuff wasn't high on my list when I could be gardening, hunting, or fishing… the latter the reason for us finding ourselves so close to the Arctic Circle.

Without speaking, Jordan opened the pack and laid everything out to get a feel for what it all was. I got the disinfectant pads out and tore them open with my teeth and handed them over to the guys as they worked.

"What's he saying?" I asked Brian.

"There was a flash of light and his radio died. Then… I think he had a heart attack. I don't know how he's still alive to be honest."

"Me neither," Jordan said, his hands flying through the supplies.

He'd used butterflies to tape a head wound closed instead of using the sutures I had in the kit. I'd ask him about that later on, but instead, I got out the plastic inflatable cast for isolating broken bones. Brian saw that and nodded. I kept it uninflated as I slowly threaded Bill's arm through it. He stiffened up and moaned. I worked slowly, gently, so it wouldn't hurt until I had his arm in there from wrist to elbow. Absently, I noticed that they were doing chest compressions again. I was about to lean over and inflate it when Jordan tapped me on the shoulder. I didn't look up until he almost pushed me over, tapping my shoulder again.

"He's gone," Jordan said.

"What?" I asked, looking up.

Bill's color had gone, almost to gray. Jordan and Brian looked sickened, and I realized I'd heard a sobbing behind me. I turned my head and saw that Tracy was there and realized I'd been hearing her soft sobs for some time.

"I... He quit breathing a minute ago and we lost him."

"Can't you keep doing CPR?" I nearly screamed.

"We did. I think he had another heart attack. The shock alone would have killed him, but look," he said pointing to Bill's chest.

I stood up, every muscle creaking in my body, my knees making a popping sound. He was pointing to the same bruised spot I'd noticed earlier.

"His pacemaker got fried somehow," Jordan said, "It was only a matter of time."

"That's not a bruise?" I asked.

"No, that's a pacemaker scar. I've seen enough of them to know. I just never..."

"He said the radio went out right before the heart attack," Brian said.

It hit me then. I'd been prepping for this exact scenario, yet here I was in the north woods of Canada, a thousand miles north of mid-Michigan where I called home. All my food, guns, and back-up plans… two hours by plane and thirteen and a half hours by car away. I pulled out my phone and it was blank. I tried the power button. I felt somebody lean into me to look and wasn't surprised to see it was Tracy, her sobs quieted.

"Do you have your phone with you?" I asked her.

"Just for taking pictures, there's no signal up here."

"Is it charged?" I asked.

She nodded and pulled hers out and flipped it open. After a moment, she handed it to me with a puzzled look on her face. I hit the power button and it didn't turn on.

"What does this mean?" she asked me.

I took a deep breath and looked around. Everybody was staring at me. One more big deep breath and I told them what I was thinking. For once, Jordan didn't mock or ridicule me.

CHAPTER 3

n EMP?" Brian asked, "Like in those dooms-day movies?" he asked.

"You said he saw a flash of light high up in the sky, then his pacemaker quit and his radio went out," I told him.

"Why didn't the plane just die?" Jordan asked.

"Remember the reason why we couldn't all come out here? The Otter is down. They fly 40 or 50-year-old airframes. The electronics in them were probably the only modern thing inside of them," I said guessing.

"That makes sense," Tracy said surprising me, "My daddy quit working on our cars in the mid-eighties when he said that the modern electronics were just too confusing. It's why he kept up his old beater until last year."

"How are we going to get home?" Brian asked, pulling Tracy into his lap.

I didn't know. We'd gone over that aspect more times in the last thirty minutes than I cared to admit.

"The company will fly another plane out here to get us, won't they?" Jordan asked.

I don't know why he was asking me, but I shook my head.

"I don't know, they were waiting on the part for the Otter. If it was an EMP, I don't think Fed-Ex is going to be delivering it anytime soon," I told them soberly, despite being on my third beer, "I think it's a wait and see type of thing."

"Wait and see? So like… What do we do?" he asked.

"Pretend this is a fishing trip, wait our two weeks. If they have somebody picking up stranded anglers, I'm sure they'll miss the first two check-ins. If they do, then we'll know for sure."

"This is not funny," Tracy said, suddenly looking at me angrily.

"I never said it was. Do you know what we have here for tools, besides what we brought?"

"There's a shed out back with a lock on it," Brian said. "Bill told us it was for maintenance supplies and stuff."

I nodded and dug in my backpack. I pulled out a small silver device that almost looked like a staple gun. I pulled out the picks and put one in the lock pick gun and gave it a few experimental clicks.

"What's that?" Jordan asked.

"Lock pick gun," I told him grabbing the tension wrench that came with it and stood.

"What are you going to do?" Brian asked me, an eyebrow raised.

"See if they have any shovels in the shed," I told them.

"Why?" Tracy asked me acidly.

"Do you want to smell Bill 2 weeks from now?" I asked her sharply.

"They're going to be here soon," she said.

"Fine, I'll dig the hole, and in three days or a week you can lay Bill to rest and fill it in," I said stomping out.

The lock pick gun is actually a pretty simple device. It's basically a master bump key that'll work on anything but a car's ignition. It doesn't weigh a whole lot and if I would have remembered that I had it in my backpack I probably would have removed it to save on weight and bring in a little more supplies. It would have probably saved me enough weight for half a dozen simple snares.

With dinner, the plane crash, and the wild trip out to the middle of the lake, I really hadn't had a chance to look around the property much. I literally went from the lake to the cabin. Following the door to the right, I went towards the back where the outhouse was and immediately saw the small shed. It was probably 8'x4' at most, sided and roofed with t-111 plywood, painted a dark green. It would blend in with the background and was hard to see in the fading light, but I was looking for it.

A simple brass lock was holding the door closed. I could probably have just removed the screws on one side and opened it, but I already had the gun out. I put it in and pulled the trigger several times and used the tension wrench on the bottom to put pressure on it. I felt the three tumblers in the lock click open when I pressed the handle on the gun one last time and was rewarded by being able to turn the keyway, clicking the lock open. I took the pick off the gun and put that and the tension wrench in my wallet so I wouldn't drop or lose them then opened the door.

Inside was shingles, old flashing, some large pieces of plywood scrap and a multitude of hand tools including several shovels, probably for digging new holes for the outhouse.

"Hey man," I heard Brian ask me, "I know we're all on edge here, but you've been real shitty about Tracy for a while now."

"What's your point?" I asked him, somewhat startled by him sneaking up on me.

"That's my wife," he said softly, anger evident in his voice.

"Shouldn't have married my ex then," I told him, something I shouldn't have had to say.

"Is that what this is about? That was like, twenty years ago; I didn't even know you then," Brian said.

I grunted. We'd worked together on some jobs, became friends. Started hanging out. By a weird twist of fate, I'd never met his wife Tracy until almost six months later and I'd realized who she was immediately. I'd been trying to play it cool and for the most part, Tracy had too, but I spent almost 17 years not even thinking about her and then suddenly she was back in my life again.

"We've been friends for a few years now, you're just now figuring this out?" I asked him, acid in my voice as I pulled a few shovels out.

Four of us, four shovels.

"Do you think burying him today is a good idea?" he asked quietly, changing the subject.

"It's what, about sixty-five, seventy degrees out today, right?" I asked him.

"Yeah, about that..."

"So," I asked, "let's say you shot a deer. How long would you leave it hanging before you decided to process it with these kind of temps?"

"Uh, I'd start processing it today," he said.

"Ok, why?" I asked him, trying to let the anger out of my voice.

"Because the meat would start to spoil right away..."

His words trailed off and he nodded. In two or three days, Bill might be a little bit on the ripe side.

"Tell you what, let's dig the hole, and we'll wait a day or so, just in case they do send somebody," Brian suggested.

"I'm ok with that. Listen, man, I'm sorry," I said and I realized I was. "We're a thousand miles from home, with no way to contact the outside world, and I'm in a cabin with my two best friends and an ex-wife I hate. I don't mean to..."

Something clicked in my chest and I sat down, putting my hand on the handle of one of the shovels as I leaned forward. I stared at my feet until I felt my emotions coming back into a semi-controlled state.

"How do you stay so calm through all of this?" I asked him.

"What do you mean?"

"Being stuck here, the EMP, pulling Bill out of the drink… I can't believe you did that, you crazy son of a bitch."

He chuckled a second and then said, "I don't know if I really have bought into the idea of an EMP, but my watch and emergency radio are dead. Maybe it was a solar flare or just something that happened right here. I'm not going to worry and buy trouble until I know there's something I need to worry about."

"You don't think having no plane to fly us back, a dead pilot and a thousand or more miles from your own house isn't a reason to panic?"

"Nope," he said and walked away.

I realized that he was compartmentalizing everything. Dealing with it one section at a time. Maybe I should do that as well.

"Need a hand?" Jordan asked me, coming up from somewhere in the direction of the outhouse.

"Sure," I said and handed him a shovel.

NORTHERN LIGHTS

For the next day and a half, we didn't do much more than catch what we needed for food so we wouldn't have to dig into our stash. The mosquitos were bad, but it was the black flies that were the worst. They swarmed all over the place, and we ended up wrapping Bill in a blue tarp I'd found in the shed to try to prevent maggots. We'd dug the hole a little further back than the shed, in a soft loamy spot near some pine trees, and dragged Bill to there.

I was sitting on the dock, looking out at nothing when I felt somebody walk up behind me. Probably Jordan coming out to try his hand at some lake trout. He'd mentioned that earlier, but I'd been brooding. Waiting for something to happen. In all the classes, YouTube videos, and my own experiences, I wasn't prepared for the reality of waiting. There was nothing that could train your mind for when the shit actually did hit the fan and you felt like you had to be doing something, but you had to wait.

If they didn't get us, how long would it take to walk 1,000 miles? It would probably be more in the end as it wasn't a straight shot and there was water to cross and all sorts of other things. I did some mental math, having no idea what would be realistic. But say I could walk ten miles a day, that would be like 100 days of walking, over three months. I didn't have three months' worth of supplies, nor could I carry three months' worth of supplies.

I could see if we could drag one of the boats to one of the numerous rivers… But many of them led to other lakes or even one of the bigger bodies of water eventually. Not where you want to be with an 18' rowboat. The only other place I could think of was the reservation. The only reason I'd noticed it was I pulled up a Google earth map showing the topography to see how far out in BFE Pringle Lake was. It was pretty far out because I had to hit the zoom button half a dozen times, but the first thing I'd seen was the reservation to the northwest of the lake. I didn't know exactly where it was, nor did I know how far it was.

In essence, I was beginning to conclude that we were fucked.

"Penny for your thoughts?" Tracy said sitting down next to me on the dock.

Shit.

"You'd have made about half a cent then," I told her and stared off into the distance.

"No, not you. You're thinking, planning. It's why you're more upset than everyone else here," she said softly.

"Well, you're about 70 percent of the reason I'm upset," I admitted. "If you weren't here I'd have about 2/3's less to gripe about," and then wondered if I'd actually said that out loud or thought it.

"I'm sorry," she said simply.

"For what?"

"For whatever it is you're blaming me for. I'm sorry, all right?" Her voice was almost pleading.

"You cheated on me," I told her.

It was the one thing that I'd never been able to tell Brian, why I hated his wife so much. He'd bugged me on more than one occasion why, other than I used to be married to her, and I just… didn't tell him. As much as I disliked her, I didn't want him to look at her the same way I did. With suspicion and disgust.

"We were twenty. I've changed. You've changed," she told me.

"I haven't changed all that much, honestly."

"So why come up here if you hate me so much?" There was something in her voice that I couldn't put my finger on… maybe hurt?

"Actually, I wasn't going to. Jordan talked me into coming. When I found out Brian was going to bring you, I tried to get a refund."

"You know what? You're still the same sad, immature boy who never grew up," she said, standing.

Maybe I was. She left just as silently as she'd come out. I stared into the water, my thoughts dark. I knew we should be doing something, executing some plan. I was almost shaking with the urge to do something, anything. Should we go? Should we stay? The cabin was outfitted with two grills; one of them was a smoker, a little Coleman wood or charcoal fired. I thought about the fish in the lake, and I thought about the dark shapes I'd seen at the water's edge a half a mile away that morning.

Moose, elk, caribou. I didn't know what they were called up here, but I supposed it was a moose in all likelihood. It had been wading into the water, its head dipping underneath and pulling something up to eat. I'd been half tempted to go see what it was that it'd been going after, but I'd remembered Bill's warning. The way my circular thinking went, I then remembered the next day was the day I was going to put Bill to rest, one way or another.

"Dude," Jordan said, sitting down next to me.

Apparently I have this big neon sign on my head that says "Tom can fix your problems, come talk to me!" or something equally stupid.

"How you doing?" I asked him.

"This thing with you and Tracy, can you stop it man?" he asked me.

"I didn't start it. I was sitting out here alone with my thoughts," I answered him, turning to the side.

He'd brought out a stringer and his steelhead rod with a spoon already set on his swivel. He cast it out before answering and began his retrieve.

"You might not have started it, but she's in there crying. Won't tell Brian what it's about. He's about ready to come out here and kick your—"

He jerked the rod hard, and I heard an exhalation of breath as he set the hook and the water swirled about fifteen feet in front of me. I could see a flash of silver scales and watched as he played the fish until it tired. By the size of the fish, I knew I should have grabbed the landing net, but I didn't feel like getting up. My feet were dangling, just touching the crystal clear water. Jordan leaned down, holding the rod up high in his left hand and pulled out a Northern Pike by the gills. He smiled at me in triumph.

"Good, dinner is served," I said dryly.

Both of us turned when we heard the screen door bang and a furious Brian came stomping in our direction. I just watched. Anger was etched into his features, but in the grand scheme of things, I didn't start it. I wasn't the one who cheated, and I wasn't the one who'd left. Tracy was. If she wanted to be upset at me, that was fine. But I'd done nothing to her nor Brian.

"What did you say to my wife?" Brian fumed, his hands forming fists.

"My *ex-wife* wanted something I couldn't give her," I told him simply, pulling my feet out of the water and using my hands to push myself into a standing position.

Brian turned a furious shade of red and he clenched his fists again. He's my buddy, not my best friend like Jordan is, but one thing I wouldn't do was take a beating sitting down if that's what he was wanting to dish out.

"Excuse me?" Brian hissed.

"Forgiveness," I told him, pushing past him abruptly.

The move surprised him, but just as fast he was surprised I was already walking. I went past the outhouse and to the shed to see what other hand tools were in there. What other supplies. I'd kept it unlocked, and it still was when I went back to it. I dug through the scraps of plywood until I found the back wall where I'd seen other handles. I found a bow saw hanging on a nail and a small axe. It wasn't a splitting axe, but if it came to that I figured I could make it work out.

I hefted the axe and right away saw the back side of it was flattened. I tossed that out the front door into the soft grass and was about to toss the bowsaw out after it so I had room to work when the light was blocked by a figure in the doorway. I turned and saw it was Brian again.

"What?" I asked him.

"What did you say to my wife?" he repeated.

"It's ancient history, man. Something that happened almost twenty years ago. It isn't what you think," I told him, not wanting to tell him the truth.

"It doesn't look like ancient history when it has her bawling," he said.

"She doesn't bawl. She sniffles. She cries. She's crying now obviously, so I dunno what to tell you, man."

"There's more to it; you've always hated her. I don't get it, man."

"You wouldn't," I answered.

He stood there in the doorway, blocking me in for a few more moments and then left with a disgusted sound. I tossed the bow saw out and kept rooting around until I found a splitting wedge. That's why the back of the axe was mushroomed out a little bit; it'd been used as a sledge. The cabin already came equipped with campfire wood, and I was sure in the winter time it was outfitted with firewood on the inside to go along with the propane wall heaters.

Since it was late July, we hadn't had to use any heat, but it did get cool at night. Much cooler than I'd expected.

"Want a hand?" Jordan asked as I was getting out of the doorway.

"Sure," I told him.

NORTHERN LIGHTS

"What are we doing?" he asked.

"Going to find some dead trees or some wind-fall then cut them up into chunks."

"What for?" he asked.

"Firewood," I told him, "and something to start smoking fish."

"You know, man, you could be wrong. Somebody could come check on us this week."

"What if I'm right?" I asked him.

He stood there for a moment and smiled. "Then it's a good thing we're cutting firewood."

CHAPTER 4

Jordan and I kept busy for the next few days. There was no airplane, and during one of our trips to gather firewood, Bill was buried by Tracy and Brian. The smell had become so rank and I was somewhat relieved, but I wasn't relieved by the tension that had built up between Tracy, Brian, and I. We'd hardly talked, and I took two days for dishes and cooking, not talking to them once. I was glad that it hadn't come to blows, and upon reflection, I'd probably done little to calm Brian down when he'd confronted me on the dock.

My mind was elsewhere quite a bit, and after eating mostly fish for a few days, I decided that it was time to do some frogging to get a different flavor with the night's meal, along with some of the food I packed with me. I didn't open the final two buckets, but both of them had a ton of dried pack food in there. One of them was half full of freeze dried stuff, and I had plans on trying to make amends over dinner.

"More firewood?" Jordan asked me as I stood to stare out at the woods.

"I was thinking about catching some frogs later on tonight," I told him. "But I also want to start up the smoker and see how good of a job it does."

"You're worried about us running out of food?" he asked, a small smile tugging the corners of his mouth.

"Yes," I said, "although I'm getting the impression that nobody is taking me seriously," I admitted.

"No, I think you're right. I mean, I checked all the electronics we all brought. They're all dead, I told you that."

"Then why does nobody believe me?" I asked.

"I do, it's just…"

"Yeah?" I asked him when his words trailed off.

"It's a pretty grim outlook, and I haven't had a chance to think about it. I mean, I am helping you lug firewood. Which reminds me, I need to do some swimming today, my back is killing me!"

I grimaced. I was probably in the poorest shape of all my friends, and if Jordan was calling uncle, I should too. Instead, I was trying to keep my shit together and figure out how to fix the uncomfortable silence that had fallen.

"My back's killing me too. Did you bring any Tylenol or anything?" I asked him, curious as he was the medical professional.

"Yeah, I have a mini kit, though it's nothing like your trauma kit. You bring stuff?"

I laughed and nodded.

"You really think we're going to be stuck up here for a while, don't you?"

"Yeah," I said sobering, "I do."

I cooked up some beans and chopped up chunks of the pike and musky that Jordan and Brian had caught. Fish chili wasn't all that hard; I'd soaked the dried beans for a couple hours, then boiled and did the water change like I normally would. Brian just watched me somewhat sullenly at first, and then with increasing interest. He seemed to be thawing out a bit and, when I fried the pike chunks and then poured the Chili over top of the big fillet pieces, he was almost drooling beside me.

"Listen, man," I said, trying to start out the conversation.

"You know what man, can we just put it between us? Bury the hatchet? I get it now, I think. You and Tracy used to have a thing and every time you see her… you kind of go back in time when you two…"

"Yeah, I'd like to just forget the other day. I don't want us all to fight, and if we don't see a plane this week we need to start planning for the winter time," I told him, starting to dish everyone's portions out onto plates.

"What are we looking at?" he asked. "I know

you studied this kind of stuff before."

He was right, I had.

"I don't know, man, I think we really need to start looking for food, firewood, and whatever we can to insulate this place. It's barely seventy degrees outside and it's July; I can't imagine what winter is going to be like."

He paused for a moment before speaking. "You think we're going to die up here, don't you?"

"I think we're going to be extremely lucky to survive the winter," I admitted. "But that's just between us, man."

"Trust me, I don't want Tracy to get worked up… God, you know how she is, better than anyone."

I couldn't help it, a wry smile cracked my stoic features and I chuckled.

"She's a good woman. We've all changed, and I think that's what's been… keeping me from seeing that in her. How much I've grown and changed. I mean, shit, it's been like 20 years," I told him.

"So what's for dessert?" I heard Tracy ask from somewhere behind us.

"Chocolate cheesecake," I said and grinned when her jaw dropped open.

"I take back every mean word I've ever said to you. Where is it?"

I'd brought the dehydrated ingredients with me. Sure, it wouldn't taste as well as the real thing would fresh, but it beat out my earlier idea of pudding. I'd save that one for later.

"Jordan's cooking it outside at the campfire. We

set up a double boiler type contraption with the Dutch oven."

Both of us were almost flung from our feet as Tracy went pushing past us. For once, she didn't look like the devil to me, just a woman who wouldn't be stopped when matters of life and death were at stake… or chocolate and cheesecake. Both interchangeable in equal parts I suppose.

"You did that on purpose…" Brian said slowly.

"I don't know how else to fix things," I said, "so I go with what I know best. Food," I told him rubbing my stomach.

He smiled and clapped me on the shoulder and went to the door, holding it open as Jordan came inside. Jordan's hands were wrapped in kitchen towels, holding the cast iron pan we'd made the cheesecake in.

"It has to cool down first," he called over his shoulder.

Tracy was pulling what looked like a Swiss army knife out of her pocket and snapped open an attachment. A fork. I had to smile.

"It's not ready for that, it has to cool. It'll just be mush now."

"It's got chocolate…" she said, her voice low and raspy.

"Dude, you didn't bring her PMS fixes?" I asked Brian, dumbfounded.

"I forgot," he said in a quiet voice. "Besides, she hates camping and we were tight on weight…"

"God, I wish I could have brought more stuff," Brian admitted, watching as his wife tried stabbing her Swiss army fork into the cheesecake as Jordan kept fumbling with it and trying to keep it away from her.

"Tracy," I said. "How about you let Jordan set that down, it's hot."

"It's chocolate cheesecake," she said as if it explained everything.

To her, it probably did. I know how to end a fight with her, I'd figured it out from her mother in the early 90s.

"I've got a few Hershey bars I was saving for s'mores in one of my buckets—"

She made one last stab for the cheesecake, and Jordan ended up tripping over his own legs as she snatched the towel wrapped handles out of his hands and let out an inarticulate cry of joy. I busted up laughing and Brian was wiping his eyes. Just like that, I felt the rampant hatred I'd nursed for years leaving me. The simple act of good-natured horseplay in what I considered to be a grim situation made me see how shallow my continued anger was. I couldn't forgive her all at once, and maybe not even completely, but it was a start.

Jordan was also laughing at this point, watching Tracy putting the cheesecake on the windowsill near the sink to cool down.

"That was... unexpected," I admitted.

"You really were trying to bury the hatchet, weren't you?"

"Yeah, I am. I think we're going to be up here a long time," I said.

Jordan had been watching and he just nodded

in agreement before adding, "that's why we've been getting all the firewood we can. I know Tom has an idea about food, but I'm worried about the cabin here."

"The cabin?" we both asked, "What's wrong with the cabin?" Brian finished as Tracy came up and stood next to him.

"It isn't insulated," Tracy said to Brian, "you'll probably have to have four times as much wood with no insulation."

"What do we do about that?" Jordan asked.

"Wait, I didn't think you believed that we're really stuck here?" I asked.

They looked at each other and then turned to me. Brian spoke, "We've been talking. Shouldn't we even see military transport planes from time to time up here?" he asked.

"Yeah, I guess we should," I admitted.

"There aren't any planes, none at all," Tracy said. "So we talked about what it'd be like up here… Living off the land."

"You hate camping," I told her, not sure if that was a question or a statement.

"It is what it is. Without a float plane, we're stuck up here anyways. We were talking about the emergency kit from the plane. If we can get that, there's a flare gun. We can probably signal to somebody if they ever do fly near here. Not all planes will have been affected, right?"

"No, most military stuff should be fine, but it's worrying that we haven't seen anything. If we knew what was going on in the rest of the world…"

"That's just it, they might be at war. We might be in the best possible place. You never know…"

"Hey, let's can the doom and gloom talk," Tracy interrupted. "Let's eat, the cheesecake will be cool by then, and we can make plans and schemes later, now that we're all getting along."

"We are, aren't we?" Brian asked.

"He brought cheesecake," Tracy said, pointing at me with the Swiss army knife. "He knows how to say sorry. You could really learn something from him."

"Oh God," Brian murmured, and we all laughed.

CHAPTER 5

The next few days had us trying to figure out what our plan of attack was. The scraps of plywood were all brought inside. The first order of business was to insulate the roof of the small 10x20 cabin. Luckily, nobody had thought to burn the building scraps and had instead left them in the shed. Most of them were squared off chunks, so of course the best ideas on how to insulate the roof fell onto… Jordan.

Yeah, it wasn't my idea but as soon as he mentioned it, I slapped my head in an *"OH MY GOD THAT'S BRILLIANT!"* type of moment. The idea was to nail the wood to the uncovered trusses and then pile in layers of leaves and pine needles from the woods. It might not be the cleanest form of insulation, but it was a good start. The problem was that we wouldn't have enough scraps to cover the entire ceiling of the cabin with wood. This is where I got my turn to shine. I found a blue tarp and, to me, the problem was solved.

That's how I ended up holding a coffee table steady as Jordan hammered in looted roofing nails from a half used up box we found near the roofing materials. Brian and Tracy were trying their hand at food production: fishing. It was ridiculously easy to catch fish, but would that change in a week? In a month? We'd been here for over a week now without anybody checking on us. The fact that nobody came for Bill was troubling as well because we were just a few tourists, and Bill was a known entity.

"Ok, I got it," Jordan said jumping down, wiping the sweat off his brow.

"Hot up there?" I asked him.

"It is now that the heat stops lower instead of going up to the roof. It's a funky looking drop ceiling. Let's get it filled by section and make sure it holds."

It took us two days to get the ceiling of the cabin covered with tarp and wood scraps and to fill it in with dried leaves and pine needles. We didn't know how much of an R value it had, so we went deep, using an old table cloth to pile up the leaves and transport them. The plastic cloth was old and cracked with age, but it was serviceable. The first day that Tracy and Brian caught way too many fish to process at once, a few spoiled before we were able to get them on the smoker. We also wasted a fair amount on the smoker, almost burning the bottom racks black before we got the hang of it.

It was going to be interesting, but we each had our own projects to figure out. We were scratching our heads over how to insulate the walls when I heard Tracy scream. Jordan took off like a shot, but I ran towards my cot and my big backpack and duffel. I took out the Henry camp gun. It was a risk bringing the gun on this trip because we weren't going to be doing any hunting really, but I didn't like to go anywhere without one. The Henry AR7 looks like the stock of a gun, but it's what's inside of the stock that makes it go 'boom'.

I pulled the butt plate off and started to assemble the gun even as I was walking out the front door… to see three bears digging through the dirt near the fish cleaning station. I had three magazines, all .22LR, but in different variations. One was loaded with rat shot, one was loaded with hollow points and one was loaded with ball ammo. That was what I put in, and I prayed I wouldn't have to actually have to use it to defend myself if push came to shove.

There was one larger bear who seemed totally unimpressed by Brian's yelling and Tracy's shrill cries. The smaller two bears, however, were looking. Tracy picked up a stick just as I put a magazine in the now assembled firearm, and racked the slide. She threw the stick from about twenty feet away and it smacked one of the smaller bears in the head, right when I realized what I was seeing. A momma bear and her two almost grown cubs.

The cub let out a yowl that made momma look up. She stood up on her hind legs, blowing and huffing at the humans who were now encroaching on her, and threatening her cubs. Her attention was not focused solely on Tracy.

"Don't do that!" I screamed from the opposite side, drawing the attention of all three.

I couldn't see Jordan; he must have gone off somewhere out of sight. I couldn't take a direct shot towards the bears because Brian and Tracy were in the crossfire, so I aimed at the ground and squeezed off a shot. The pop was loud and a small amount of dirt kicked up at my feet. It had an effect, though. All three bears startled and the mother dropped to all fours. She was walking backward and to the side, keeping the lake to her right flank as she backed up.

The cub let out a squall and as I was turning to take aim just in case they turned in ran. Feeling smug, I held up my little rifle letting out a battle cry of my own, realizing that everyone had been screaming. Except I hadn't noticed who was screaming behind me. I turned and saw that Jordan was advancing from behind the cabin, running with a long oar, probably a backup from the shed, shrieking like a banshee. The three of us turned and watched as he ran towards the bears, screaming his fool head off. They lumbered away slowly and barely gave him a look. He stopped near the dock panting, and put the handle of the oar on the ground and leaned on it, his chest heaving.

"Are you ok?" I yelled loudly.

"I'm good. You ok, Tom?" Tracy yelled back.

I nodded. We all were walking towards the dock, where Jordan wearily leaned on the oar. I knew he was feeling the adrenaline dump because the danger was over yet he was still shaking. Hell, I was starting to get the shakes. I made sure the AR-7 was on safe and put it on the picnic table as I passed it.

"What were you thinking?!" Brian asked as I drew near.

"I was trying to scare it off. It worked, obviously," she chided.

"My shot scared them off," I added.

"You're all wrong, didn't you listen to Bill about what to do in a bear attack or a near bear attack?" Jordan asked, exasperatedly.

"Lay down and pretend you're a chicken nugget?" Tracy asked sweetly and batted her eyelashes.

That broke the tension and we laughed for a good bit. As they started retelling the bear story to each other, I went to the cleaning station where the bears had been and frowned. The bears had turned over the dirt in a couple of places, and I could see fish scales and bits and pieces of fish. Instead of bagging the offal and taking it far off to dump elsewhere when they were cleaning fish, they had just dug a hole next to the cleaning station and buried the guts and heads.

"Hey, Brian," I called, and in a moment, he was beside me.

"Remember how they said not to keep food

outside and close to the cabin?" I asked him, sort of pissed.

I mean, would the bears be back later on? Now that they knew where the food was, they were bound to come back and a mother with cubs was supposed to be a fearsome critter. I had no doubt that my little .22 would merely piss it off, but the report had clearly startled it, no matter how scary Jordan thought he looked waving that oar around.

"Oh, man," Brian said. "That's my fault. It was getting dark and I was going to dig that up and move it later today."

"We should do it before it gets dark," I said. "This could have been really ugly."

Jordan and Tracy stepped in close to look at the hole the bears had dug up, and then to us.

"They were just going for the easier meal," Jordan observed.

"Let's dump the guts far down the shoreline," Tracy suggested. "Get them going somewhere else."

"I don't know if it's worth using the gas, but I'm all for that, for a while at least," Brian said. "We only have so much gas, and if we're really caught out here…"

"We have to make it last," I said, "but it won't last forever. Gas goes bad over time."

"What would you suggest?" Tracy asked.

"Make your husband get a shovel and a bucket…"

BOYD CRAVEN

It became apparent to us rather quickly that fish jerky would be easy to make, but without salt or seasoning it would definitely be difficult to make it all winter on that alone. I'd started dreaming of hamburgers early on when I'd realized I probably wouldn't have another. Gradually, a big chunk of meat became something I desperately wanted to get my hands on. In theory, my .22 could drop a moose or caribou or whatever, with the proper placement. I didn't trust myself to do that so I started scheming ways of trapping them. Going back to my roots as a kid. The problem was I didn't have any snares big enough, nor heavy duty enough. to take down any sort of large game.

I was staring out at the water again, sitting on the end of the dock when it came to me. The airplane. It was full of cables and parts we could use. The controls on the small Cessnas were all cable driven, and the plane had only been in the water a week. If we were lucky, corrosion wouldn't have set in yet.

"Penny for your thoughts?" Tracy asked, sneaking up behind me again.

"I want a burger," I admitted, "and I'm scheming ways to get some. Or a mooseburger. Something. I just…" I broke off and looked up at the sky. I could feel the dock move as more people stepped out, and I saw the guys heading towards us.

"Pop a squat," I offered and she did, putting her bare feet in the water.

"How's it going?" I asked Brian as he got close.

"Latest batch of fish is on the smoker. We're

good for a while. I was wondering what you were thinking?" Brian asked me.

"Why does everyone suddenly care what I'm thinking?" I asked, curious.

"We're now on what, day 9 and haven't seen a plane..." Jordan said. "And you're the one with a plan for this sort of situation."

"I don't have a plan exactly," I admitted, "but I've given this stuff a lot of thought."

"Well, we have about a week's worth of fish jerky," Tracy said, "but I don't know how long it'll last in the cabin, and I don't trust leaving it outside of the cabin because those bears might come back..."

"Isn't there a trapdoor by the back door?" I asked them.

Jordan nodded. "I checked that out actually. It's part of the cistern system. I'm sure they pump the cistern full from the lake once in a while, filter it or treat it... But the plumbing access is down there."

"But the sink runs on a hand pump," Tracy said.

"Water's water, tank, ground, well..." Her husband said, sitting behind her, wrapping her in his arms. "You have to pump it to where you want it. Hand pump, solar pump, electric pump..."

"Ok, but what's that got to do with anything?" Jordan asked me.

"Can we get to the dirt, or is it cement down there?" I asked.

"It's dirt. The whole place was built over a footing and cement block with a dirt floor. There're some layers of visqueen down there but..."

"That's perfect," I told him, "Let's check it out!"

We followed Jordan over to the trapdoor that led to the access and dropped down. I was surprised when he went almost waist deep to the floor. He crouched lower and disappeared. I followed him down. Immediately I crouched and tried to see around in the dark. Thankfully, the footing wasn't poured concrete, it was cinder blocks on top of whatever footing material they'd used. It was what we'd call a Michigan basement or half basement. Set into the cinder block were two glass block casement-sized windows, illuminating parts of the basement.

Cobwebs brushed against my face as I crawled out of the way and Brian poked his head down into the hole.

"There's a lot of room down here," he said.

"Cistern tank is really close to the trapdoor. What do you think if we dug something over here?" I asked, pointing.

"That'd work, what would we use to line it with?" Brian asked me.

"What are you guys talking about?" Jordan asked, crawling back towards us on his hands and knees.

"Going to dig a hole in the damp soil here, use one of the trash cans and then bury it up to the lid. We can start putting the jerky into some of those clear bags they left us for fish guts, and then put them in the can. It'd stay what, 55-60 degrees at the most?" Brian asked me, obviously catching on to my idea.

NORTHERN LIGHTS

"Yeah, that's pretty much what I was thinking," I admitted. "But we have to do more than just fish. If I don't get a Big Mac sometime soon, I might just go crazy." I said smiling.

"Too bad there aren't any cows around here," Jordan said. "I know we're trying to stretch our supplies, but I'm getting sick of fish."

"The horror," Tracy teased. "The fishing trip isn't even over yet. Besides, I think Tom has a scheme in his head on how to get the burger. Don't you Tom?"

My grin was big and wide. "You guys are going to love this."

Their groans were long and loud. I barely held in a belly laugh.

CHAPTER 6

Of course, I'd packed about 8 pounds of books for the trip and about half of that was dedicated to foraging and what edible plants were available in Michigan. I knew a lot of it by heart, but we were in Canada; close enough but there were some things that I was sure were different. I couldn't be the only one with the knowledge, though, it had to be spread out. And so, my nefarious plans for getting a burger, or, at least, a steak burger, were hatched.

In my dried food storage, I had packed in a small amount of flour, baking soda, baking powder, some yeast, and a 2# pack of cornmeal. We would quickly run out of flour to make bread, but I had another idea, one I thought would be perfect since it was summer, and things ran a little later in the season than they did back home.

"You want me to shake the pollen out of the cat-tails?" Tracy asked dubiously.

"Yeah, and then dig it up, roots and all. Cut off the roots and bring those back too!"

"You're so weird," Tracy said after a second and left, not quite stomping.

"Is that busy work, or is it really going to help us out?" Brian asked, watching his wife leaving with amusement.

"No, it'll work. I haven't done it myself, but I've read about it. I haven't seen any acorns around here, you can make flour with those too you know?"

"I've heard. Hey, wouldn't it be smart for us to collect those also? Nuts I mean?"

"There's too many in this shack already," Jordan said, "And the smoker is overflowing again. We gotta do something about that, man."

He was right, we did. We ended up washing and hosing out the big garbage cans and burying them like we had planned. Tracy, being the smallest in the group, was not happy with her task of having to crawl inside of the large (supposedly) bear-proof bins and hit them with a rag and soapy water. She came out quite a sight and, I must admit, I laughed until she threatened my very existence. Since the end of our fishing trip had arrived and passed, and there was still no plane, reality had kicked in and we'd all talked about projects that needed to be done.

I explained about salvaging everything we could from the plane and the broken wing sections. I was hoping to gain a few hundred feet of heavy cable, the first aid kit, the emergency kit, and if they could locate it, the emergency beacon. Like Bill's rescue, it would mean all of us going out; one to run the boat, two to dive and get supplies and the third for relief or rescue. Since I was the best at keeping the boat in place, I had been designated the man for holding the boat in one spot.

Did I mention the water was cold? That's why we'd been waiting to dive and get all that we could. When the thermometer hit what looked like 78 degrees – which happily had not exploded with the EMP, it's mercury happily mocking the technology of the world – it was time to go.

"What are we going to do while we wait on her?" Jordan asked, looking longingly at the lake.

"I want to build a bigger smoker, maybe make a solar dehydrator too," I admitted.

"You know how to do that, or is that something you learned in a book?" Brian asked.

This time, I did in fact know firsthand. I'd done both in a workshop.

"I know how to do it, I did it in the prepper camp in the Carolinas last fall," I told them.

"Really? So what do we need?"

"I'd like to build the dehydrator first. Maybe see if we can get the fish even drier, then start on the new smoker. I think we'd be best off by first taking the screens off from the storm windows and making a box fit those," I said.

"Wait, then that would let the bugs in," Jordan was about to cry, I know it.

NORTHERN LIGHTS

"Well, then close the windows," I told him.

"Then it'll get hot," Brian griped.

Bunch of pansies.

"Ok, but we need the screens. Also, we need at least one of those layers of visqueen that's in the crawlspace," I told him.

"What do you have in mind?" Jordan asked.

The plan was pretty easy. The great thing was it would only use four nails per shelf. We still had a ton of nails left, but there would be no more once we used them up…

"We drive four poles into the ground," I told them. "Spaced so we can fit a screen inside of it. We run a piece of wood from front to back and then rest the screens on top of them like an oven rack. Then we wrap the whole thing in plastic to raise the temperature. Cut a hole in the top to let out heat and moisture and voilà."

"What's going to keep the bugs out of it?" Jordan asked.

I opened my mouth and closed it. The top hole would be a problem, the box I'd made was out of plywood on at least 1 side and the top/bottom. I'd stapled screen material across it. I wouldn't have that here unless…

"We'll lay a screen across the top," I told him, "where the vent hole goes. Ants might be the only thing we have to worry about, but if we use it on sunny days, the heat should keep them out."

"What can you dry out on one of those things?" Brian asked.

"Just about anything."

"And how are we going to do the smoker one?" Jordan asked me. "I mean, we're probably going to be using up all of the screens."

"We'll make it the same way, except we'll use some of our natural resources for making the shelf," I told them.

"How's that?" Brian asked.

"Remember how I asked Tracy to cut the roots from the stalks?" I asked them.

Realization lit both of their faces and they smiled.

"Isn't this sort of crazy?" Jordan asked.

"What do you mean?" Brian piped in.

"The world might be at war, but I'm having the time of my life," he answered.

"Have the time of your life after you take a swim, you're ripe," I said not wanting to get lost in the flow of conversation.

Holding the boat steady wasn't hard. Usually, the wind made a small chop across the lake, but it was unusually calm and once again I could see straight to the bottom. Tracy and Brian were underwater, using my multi-tool to cut loose a piece of cable. It wasn't the ideal cutter, but it was what I had handy. I got all the way out in the middle of the lake with everyone, and I realized I'd forgotten to grab my cable cutters. Maybe I could be called a freak for taking some of my trapping supplies and tools, I probably should have packed in more food… but it was what I had on me.

"Do you think building a bigger snare will be able to take down a moose?" Jordan asked me.

"Maybe a cow," I said. "A bull's antlers would be hard to fit through any sort of hoop."

"What about a leg hold type snare?" he asked me.

I stopped to consider it. I'd used leg hold traps, but every snare I'd ever used was a kill snare. Not because I thought leg holds were unethical, but it was how I learned and, when an animal breaks a snare from its anchor point, it would still fall, often within sight of the tree you anchored the snare from. Luckily I had a small tackle box of parts with me, not much, but I was thankful I'd packed my cam locks.

"That might actually work," I admitted. "But I think there'd be a bigger chance of it breaking the anchor and getting away. If I go out for one, I want it down. I want some burgers," I said.

"In case you haven't noticed, you're losing weight. These two weeks of fish and beans has slimmed you down a little bit, buddy."

I looked down, and sure enough, there was a very small difference – but the only way I noticed was because I'd cinched my belt one more notch than the normal worn out one that held up my pants.

"A little bit, I had a lot to lose, though," I admitted.

I watched as a stream of bubbles broke the surface next to the front of the boat, and Tracy came up next to Brian who was holding the end of a frayed cable in one hand and my multi-tool in the other. I took the multi-tool as they took deep breaths and passed me the end of the frayed cable.

"It should be loose. Just have to reel it in now," Tracy said with a smile.

God, she was the devil; how could I have ever married and lost her? Why wasn't I good enough?

I started to pull slowly, some tension on the cable. It came slowly and Brian dived to help guide it out easier. We'd all talked about being extra careful of getting cut on the sharp edges of the broken wing and fuselage. I was surprised when I pulled out a section of cable and realized I'd made a dozen loops on the floor and there was more still to come. It wasn't the 7x7 wire like I usually used, but if I stripped one of the bigger strands out, that would be about the same size as my 7x7 and I could make my kill snare from that and an intact section of cable for my anchor point.

"I'll be right back," Jordan told Tracy and dove deep.

"I can't believe this worked," she said. "You really think you can catch something with all this line?" Tracy asked me.

"Yeah, I do. I don't think it'll be a big deal, but we'll see," I admitted.

"I always hated your hunting and camping stuff, you know... But now it looks like that's going to save us," she said.

"There's no way I could do all of this on my own," I told her.

NORTHERN LIGHTS

"Hold on, my turn," She took a breath and dove as the other two broke the surface. I felt the line tense as Tracy took a hold of it from the bottom and then I felt the slack so I kept reeling in the cable.

"First aid kit, and I think this little black duffel is either his underwear or the emergency kit," Brian told me, tossing them into the boat.

"Anything else of use in there?" I asked them.

"Fire extinguisher," Jordan answered.

"Grab anything not nailed down," I said, using the cable to keep me over the plane instead of the big oar or motor like I'd planned.

"You got it," Brian said and they both dove.

I could feel it when the end of the cable was released from the plane because the tension on it was gone. I finished reeling it in and felt the back end of the boat dip as I got the loops in a straight line.

"Little help back here?" Tracy asked.

She didn't have the same upper body strength as the rest of us, and I know it must have cost her a lot to ask for help, especially from me. I made my way back slowly and gave her my hands and pulled. She got most of the way up and then put one knee over the edge. She tried to swing her other leg over as she straightened but was off balance. She fell forward, tripping me across an aluminum seat and landed right on top of me. My breath left me in one fast whoosh.

"Oh God, are you ok?" Tracy asked, trying to lever herself off of me.

I held up my hand to motion just a second to her as my breath came back in a rush.

"Yeah, it's just that you knocked the wind out of me," I said, my voice coming out wheezy.

"Are you implying I'm fat?" she asked, her eyes suddenly going cloudy.

"No, just that you knocked the wind out of me. What'd you hit me with, your knee?" I asked, rubbing the sore spot as she finally found her footing and moved back half a step to give me room.

"My ass," she said, and her lips were razor thin.

"Well, your ass knocked the wind out of me, I'm ok now," I said. "Give me a hand."

The combination of falling on the aluminum seat with the small of my back and having Tracy fall on top of me had left me doing nothing more than avoiding death. My lower back was killing me worse than ever, though it had been going away the more and more I swam. Tracy held out a hand and I took it, trying to get to my feet stiffly.

"So you have a problem with my ass?" she hissed.

"Never did before," I said, starting to rise to my feet.

Funny thing happened, funny for everyone but me. As Tracy was pulling me up, she kept pulling until I found myself going over the side of the boat. The shock of the cold water almost knocked the breath out of me again, and I was only too happy to make it back to the air. I looked up, pissed because I hadn't been implying anything and...

Laughter? I swam over to the edge of the boat and saw that both Jordan and Brian were working their way in by the transom and everyone was laughing, including Tracy.

"Lighten up," she said amidst the giggles, "just because it's the end of the world, it doesn't mean we can't have fun."

I thought about splashing her, but she was already wet. Instead, I held onto the side of the boat and pulled my shoes off with one hand and tossed those in. Once Jordan was in and clear, I pulled myself in. I had to give everyone credit, it was a lot harder than they'd made it look. I managed to get in the boat without tipping it, which was a win and took my spot.

"Why so serious?" Jordan said in a voice reminiscent of the Joker when Heath Ledger played him in the movie.

"I'm not, I just... If it was anybody else..." I let my words trail off and Tracy's smile faded.

"Come on man, don't give her grief, she was just playing around," Brian said, getting serious himself.

"Oh, it's not that," I said with a grin, "if it was anybody else I would have tossed you back in the water. Since it's Tracy that'd be too easy. Now I just have to find something else to do... say a snake in her sleeping bag or a spider under her coffee cup..."

"You wouldn't?!" she said in a loud shrill voice.

"Oh yes, I'm pretty sure he would," Jordan said.

Nefarious plans were coming together in my mind, and no, I decided I wouldn't scare her with a critter or two. She would imagine me doing something worse and it would build until she exploded with worry. In fact, I thought that would be even more fun than the actual prank, the buildup. I grinned evilly.

"Yeah," Brian said, "Tom's known for his pranks, hun, you'll just have to see what he comes up with. No matter what it is, it's going to be epic," he said noting my grin.

"You're dead to me," Tracy pointed at her husband.

"Hey guys, look at that!" Jordan said pointing excitedly.

Three bears were half a mile from our campsite, pushing at something in the brush. It was the same spot where we'd been dumping the fish offal. We'd decided that since the bears knew where we were, we'd keep dumping in roughly the same spot as an incentive to keep them away from us, the smokers and the dehydrator we'd just built.

"Momma bear is back," Brian said, "I wonder what they taste like?"

"I've never tried bear," I admitted.

"I have," Tracy said, surprising us all, "it was on that wild game dinner at your church. The one your grandpa invited you too."

"Oh God, I remember that," I said, "Yeah, the only ladies there were the church volunteers. I don't think you heard or cared that it was a guy's thing."

"Your grandpa was amused, that's for sure," Tracy said.

"What was it like?" Brian asked, obviously uncomfortable with the situation.

As well as he should have been I guess. He was my buddy, but he was the one who'd brought his wife, my ex-wife, on the trip, where we'd been staying in a small space. We had a shared history, and it kept popping up. Having her come probably saved her life, though, because otherwise she'd have been stuck back in Detroit somewhere alone when the grid went down. From what I'd read, societal collapse in other countries has always brought out the worst in humans, and it was the women and children who suffered first. So, I figured at least Brian could deal with his discomfort and rest easy knowing his wife was alive and safe. Even though we were all stranded in the middle of nowhere.

"It was good, a little... greasy? Not gross, but the texture was like... I don't know. If you stewed a big chunk of ham? It could have been the way it was cooked too. I also tried Elk while we were there. It didn't taste like the venison you bring home," she said putting a hand on her husband's shoulder and giving it a squeeze.

I watched the bears, listening in, but an idea was forming. It would totally be crazy, but we had nothing to lose.

"Ready to go back in?" Jordan asked, "I want to see how the new dehydrator is working."

"Sure, let's go," I said pulling the cord on the little motor.

CHAPTER 7

The new smoker we built worked, though not as great as I had hoped. The bottom two racks were too close to the heat and cooked the food too much. What the remaining shelves did, though, was quadruple our capacity to where we could put away so much fish that it was unbelievable. How we used the big smoker was a bit different than the little Coleman model, though... We worried about melting the plastic sides so, instead of building a big fire inside it, we dug a hole in the dirt and then made a fire in the fire ring outside. When it burned down into hot coals, we filled the tin bucket from the woodstove inside and ferried them into the hole in the ground. Then we added water soaked wood chips to the top. We added hot coals and chips at intervals to keep it going.

NORTHERN LIGHTS

The smoke that came billowing out was more than I expected the first time, and before we figured out how long it took before we had to rotate the meat on the shelves, we did waste some food. We also got to up our fishing routine. Instead of smoking the fish to completion, we found out we could smoke the fish for half the usual time and then put it in the dehydrator we built to finish drying off.

"That's too simple," Tracy said walking up to me.

"What is?" I asked her.

"The doors on those, hell, those are simple too, but they work. Where did you learn to do this kind of stuff?" she asked.

Instead of a hinge, I just clipped the plastic to a long stick. It was pulled across the fourth panel around the stick driven into the ground and tucked behind the pole driven into the ground and a small length of cord tied the top sticks together. Simple, primitive, but it was what we had. Bonus was the fact it was so easy to make. If the plastic didn't work, we could fashion something else… as it was…

"Well," I said, "I spent a lot of time as a kid hunting and fishing. Once I got on the prepper kick a few years back, I did a lot of reading. I started to go to workshops, the last one being in South Carolina. I built a solar dehydrator, which is basically a solar oven with a vent hole."

"What are you worried is going to happen?" she asked. "The end of the world? Y2K? That whole 2012 Mayan calendar thing?"

"It already happened," I said, confused. "We're

stuck up here because it happened."

"I know, I was just being goofy," she told me.

"Well, be goofy all you want, just don't forget to shake your boots out in the morning."

"You wouldn't dare..."

I just laughed and she stomped away, swearing vile threats, carrying a load of cattail stalks and roots inside the cabin. I knew she really wasn't pissed, but it was funny. I had no plans of putting any sort of critter anywhere near her. The last time I'd pranked her like that I'd ended up kicked in the nuts, so I wasn't about to risk actually doing it. Threatening on the other hand...

"That thing's working pretty good now," Jordan said, dragging some dead wood towards the side of the cabin to be cut and split for firewood.

"Yeah, using the cabin's thermometer made all the difference in the world now we have things figured out," I told him.

"Any luck on mooseburgers or bear burgers?"

"I'm going to be building some bigger snares tonight; want to learn how?" I asked him.

"Hey, I want to learn too!" I heard from within the cabin.

"Don't worry Tracy, you know where I live nowadays," I called back.

"Yeah, and now I know where to serve the papers!"

"Papers?" I called back, my voice echoing.

"20 years of missed alimony payments."

I sputtered for half a second and then resolved myself to actually think of a plan I could get away with up here. A prank worthy enough to pay her back for getting chucked off the boat and soaking my clothing and shoes. That was another worry, what would we do in the middle of winter time? Could we make our own leather? I had a couple binders chocked full of info. It was condensed and shrunk down literature I'd pulled off the internet and laminated, before putting them in clear plastic sleeves so I wouldn't have to poke holes through them.

I was sure I knew at least two different ways of making leather... something to do with battery acid, brain tanning and something else. I'd have to take a look.

"You wish," I called back to her.

"No, that's me wishing," Brian said walking up to the picnic table where he kept the cutting board and fillet knife.

We'd all gotten very quick and proficient with the knife. It would have horrified any fish and game wardens had they seen how many fish we were cleaning and putting away a day, but the fishing was good, and we were drying them out until they were almost brittle. We didn't seal the bags tightly, hoping that any remaining moisture could leave the bag and not mold the food. That was the hope. None of us knew what it'd be like in the wintertime. We could only guess.

"Do you think your camp gun can take down a moose?" Jordan asked.

"Hit anything in the right spot, you can kill it. Remember the story of David and Goliath?"

"Yeah, the bible story, right? Killed the giant with a sling and a rock," Jordan answered.

"Yup. The only thing that worries me is I only have a few hundred rounds of ammunition, and I'm not sure that I'm a good enough shot to hit them in the eye or..."

"What about the side of the neck, back of the head?" Jordan interrupted, "I've seen you take some really difficult shots at the range. I know hunting is different, hell my hands shake about every time I draw on a deer, but I don't know your gun and you're pretty decent with it from what I saw."

"Yeah, I guess I could, but I'd rather not wound the animal if I miss, you know?" I admitted.

"I'd rather you take a half-assed, well-practiced shot than starve to death this winter," Jordan shot back, and I shut up.

He had a point. I'd always had it drilled into my head that a .22 was a squirrel only gun or for small game like rabbit or chipmunk, despite having a ton of different shells for it. I went silent and started thinking. There was a book I read about a guy named Heimo Korth who lived somewhere in Alaska. He'd used a .22 for just about everything except bear.

"You're right, I remember reading about this guy who used a .22 on almost everything. I was thinking, yeah, he's pretty hardcore and he's way the hell up in Alaska."

"We're way the hell up north, in Canada," Jordan said, what's the difference?"

"You're right. That shot would shatter the spinal

column, and I've got some good loads I brought up with me."

"What are we going to do with all the meat?"

I thought about that and looked at the smoker and then the dehydrator. Dried meat was a staple of the American Indians. They made smoked jerky, kind of the same way we were doing it, just a little more primitive. They would build racks and start a smoky fire beneath the racks and put big thin strips of meat across the rack and let the smoke, heat, wind, and the sun dry the meat out until it was brittle, usually two or three days. The trick was not to let the heat get so hot that the food was actually cooking but to just dry it out. The smoke coated the meat so the flies wouldn't lay eggs on them, and it added flavor.

"Same thing we're doing with the fish," I said, "Smoke it, dry it, fry it up fresh."

"You want a steak burger, don't you?"

"Yeah," I admitted, "I really do."

"Hey, Grizzly Adams, come check out this flour!"

I brushed my hands off and walked towards the cabin. When I got in, I saw that Tracy and Jordan had cleared out the large area of the cabin floor, pushing the table against the wall with the chairs stacked on top of it. I knew Brian had been working on the cattail roots, and Tracy had been taking the thin stalks in for some project she had in mind. She wasn't talking but this was the first time I had been invited in. I know she got embarrassed if she tried to do a project and it failed, but asking me to stay out had me thinking at first that she was setting me up for an elaborate prank.

What I found, though, was a bit mind blowing. Tracy was sitting on the floor while Brian was working on a pot full of boiling roots. He was boiling the starch out of the roots, where we'd mash them up roughly and let things simmer and dry out the white paste and grind it into flour. What Tracy had done… Oh boy. My mind was blown.

A long mat had been made out of the stalks of the cattails. She'd weaved a panel at least six feet tall and six feet long.

"Pretty cool huh?"

"Privacy wall?" I asked her, noting that the stalks of the cat-tails looked like some sort of elaborate fancy craft creation people would pay hundreds or thousands of dollars for.

"Well, maybe eventually. See, we ran out of stuff to insulate the wall. We make panels like this and then stuff the leaves behind them…"

"That's brilliant," Jordan said from behind me.

"That's pretty awesome," I admitted.

She stood and stretched, her hands brushing the low ceiling of the cabin, making the leaves above it rustle. Brian put his spoon down and pulled her into a big hug and kissed the top of her head.

"Do you think it'll work?" she asked me.

"Yeah, I think it will," I said, walking over.

The edges were of course loose to some extent, but the ends had been cut off with a knife so it looked even, manmade.

"Help me stand it up," she said.

NORTHERN LIGHTS

I expected it to flop around and was surprised it was pretty stiff. We stood it up easily.

"Don't just stand there, Jordan," Brian scolded. "Go get the hammer."

Jordan flipped him the bird and went to the sink, where we'd stored some of the more commonly used tools and knives. Six nails later, we had it tacked into the middle. We left the top loose to make stuffing leaves in the space between the wall studs easier, and the panel almost reached the top of the uninsulated wall.

"We've got room to move the table back now," I told Jordan who was fixing to walk back out the doorway.

"All right, all right," he took one end, I took another, and we moved it back in place.

"You're going to have to move that when we start bringing in leaves," Tracy told me.

Jordan shot me a triumphant look. "Don't take this the wrong way man, but I've got a project I want to check out. She needs that table moved again…"

"No worries," Brian told Jordan. "I'll give him a hand if he gets overzealous."

"You better shake your shoes out in the morning too," I said pointing to Brian and walked out, listening to Tracy cackle.

"You want to come along?" Jordan asked me.

"Let me build up the fire a little so we can add coals in a bit."

"Sure, you got your camp gun with you?"

"In my pack, will we need it?" I asked him, my interest piqued.

"I don't know, it wouldn't hurt, I mean, we're in the middle of nowhere."

"Ok," I added a few logs to the campfire ring, so I'd have hot coals for the smoker and then got my gun out.

I put it together, Jordan watching me constantly.

"What kind of ammunition do you have in it?" he asked.

"I was going to load hollow points, but I have ball ammo if you think we're going to be scaring up something bigger.

"No, I was just wondering."

He led me to the northwestern side of the lake, past where we'd been dumping the fish guts. I was nervous walking through the area, but once we were passed it, I started to relax a bit. The woods opened up a little, the trees not so close together, and then a hillside meadow opened up before us. It'd taken us a good hour to walk there, but the view was spectacular. The sunlight hit the lake, turning it into a sheet of undulating gold, its rays reflecting almost white. In all, I wasn't sure the day could have gotten much better. Until it did.

"You're looking the wrong way," Jordan said.

I turned around to find him crouched in some low bushes that came up almost past his knees. I looked at him, puzzled.

"What is it?"

"You still have those clear plastic bags in your

daypack?" He asked me.

I nodded and pulled one out, handing it to him. He nodded and reached into the bushes. Curious, I watched as his hands moved, picking something. He held his hand out and I showed him my upraised palm. A small handful of blueberries dropped into my palm.

"What, how…?" I asked.

"My parents' had some of these growing wild when I lived in Wisconsin. I knew they had blueberries up here, but I wasn't sure that's what these were. I caught sight of the opening when we were pulling the cable up from the plane and the boat drifted while you were… swimming," he said with a grin.

I popped one into my mouth and puckered. It was sour.

"These… are kind of awful," I told him, giving him a few to try.

"Not fully ripe," he said, "I wanted to see if they were almost done. If we wait till they are full on ripe, we're going to have every bird in Canada landing here eating all of these up."

"What's the good of eating these if they taste like crap?" I asked, smiling.

We'd need something, anything, for the vitamin C. I'd read that you could get a good source of that from the liver of some animals and organ meats, but I didn't want to test that out. So much of what I knew was from books and not a lot of practical knowledge. I really wished I wasn't such a Mall Ninja sometimes.

"I think in a week or two they will be just about ready. I haven't been keeping up with the dates, but it's got to be almost August now."

"Yeah, it is," I said.

"See, it's not just the winter months we need to survive," Jordan said, "If it's anything like Northern Wisconsin, the spring weather you are used to doesn't start until May or June."

"So you think we're not putting up enough food?" I asked him.

"I think we're going to run out of place to store all the food we're putting up, and I'm worried that we're going to still run low. If the ice doesn't break up, how are we going to fish? I don't know how much the traps are going to bring in because we've yet to set them. I know winter time is supposed to be big for it—"

I cut him off, he was rambling and his words were coming out in a rush. I knew the tension and worry had built up in all of us. Our fly-in was over, and yet we were still stuck out in the middle of nowhere. I guess the reality of the situation had begun to sink in. Maybe that's why Tracy had finally gotten on board with things where at first she was skeptical.

"Dude," I said, "If you think they are ripe enough now, let's go ahead," I told him, leaning the AR-7 against a tree at the edge of the field.

A flash of relief flooded his features and I just gave him the nod and kneeled down next to him, pulling out a clear bag of my own from my daypack.

"If they aren't dark blue/purple, don't pick them.

NORTHERN LIGHTS

It would suck to have to come find and pick these in the middle of winter, so just don't."

"Will there be any left in the middle of the winter? Won't the birds get them all?" I asked.

"No, the ones that ripen too late in the season are usually safe. There probably won't be that many, though. Bears like these as well, so when they are ripe, the bears are probably going to be out in full force so that's why I think now would be a great time."

"Makes perfect sense," I told him.

I started picking. After a while, I realized that there was something calming and serene about moving about, pulling the berries and putting them into the bag. It wasn't the soft sounds of the birds calling to each other, nor the wind rustling the leaves and pine boughs of the trees on either edge of the hillside meadow. We were gathering our own food, and we were actually living the life that I'd only read about in books.

My side of the mountain, Hatchet, the non-fiction stuff about the guy in Alaska, the Grizzly man… The other thing I'd noticed was how much more I was pulling up my pants. In two weeks I'd lost probably mostly water weight, but I'd been living on a diet of rice, fish and, once in a while, biscuits from my dwindling supply of flour. We'd used it sparingly because we were gathering enough starch from the cattail roots to see if it would make a difference or give us digestive issues.

"What are you thinking man?" Jordan asked me after a while.

"To be honest, I think you'd think I was crazy if I told you," I admitted.

"No, hit me with it," he said.

"We're stuck up here right now. Something Earth-shattering has happened to the nation, maybe the world, and all I can think is… Damn, this is fun and it's the life I always kind of wanted to live."

The admission was out, and my cheeks burned with embarrassment. What I thought of as fun wasn't what everybody else probably did. I'd always wanted to live off the land, live in the rough and wild. I'd been unable to do that with my real life problems weighing me down, so much of what I knew was theoretical or from books and didn't have a big basis in real life. Almost everything I'd tried out though had worked. Tracy's experiment with the thatch style wall worked. The smoker and dehydrator worked. The insulation would work. We could do this, we could survive.

"That doesn't sound so crazy, man. There's only two things missing from my life now, that'd make it perfect." Jordan told me.

"Oh yeah? What's that?" I asked, curious and relieved that I wasn't so far out there.

"That there are no women around here, and no, Tracy doesn't count… and I'd like another ten cases of beer."

I laughed, startling a small group of birds into flight. Jordan stood up with almost a quarter of the five-gallon bag full. I stood and stretched, feeling the tendons popping in my joints. My bag had just a little bit more in it, but I'd gone about it with a mindless determination, letting my thoughts wander and my hands do the work.

"How you want to preserve these?" Jordan asked.

"Dehydrate them tomorrow, make raisins out of them?" I asked him.

"Sounds good to me. Let's go back before it gets dark. It was a long walk."

"Yup," I agreed.

It had been a long walk, but it had been made easier by game trails that ran the water's edge. If we had been going through heavy brush, it never would have been as quick, but we'd been lucky so far this trip. I hoped our luck would hold out for a while longer, or maybe all winter. I knew that probably wasn't possible, but so far, Murphy of Murphy's law hadn't reared his ugly mug. Hopefully, he was still stuck back in Michigan, having missed the trip completely. One could hope, anyway.

CHAPTER 8

The first batch of blueberry raisins wasn't done enough, so I put the screen door try back in the top of the dehydrator. The berries had some real pucker power, but something in my body ached as I put them away and shut the door again. My body seemed to want them. I knew that eating too many at once, especially if they weren't ripe, might give me digestive issues so I settled for a small handful as a sample.

We'd sort of let the firewood gathering go, because of food and other projects, so Jordan and Brian were on firewood duty to catch up. We had no idea what the R value of the now insulated walls and ceiling would be, and no way to guess how much firewood we'd need inside the cabin during the winter months. We did know what it took to keep the smoker going all day, so we used that as an estimate and figured on doubling or tripling that.

Even then, it might not be enough, so we were going to stack up three sides of the cabin and start stacking inside the cabin when things got cold outside, and make more room as we went. I'd lost track of time, but I guessed that it was August. It had gotten cool at night, enough that we were almost ready to light a fire to take out the chill, but every one of us felt the ache from cutting and splitting firewood. It was a resource that we didn't want to waste.

Tracy had left on her own with the shovel for more cattails. I'd given her the AR-7 after showing her the basics. I was on my own and, for once, I felt the pangs of loneliness. When we'd rented the cabin for the fly-in trip, the brochure had said there was a trail that leads on almost half a mile portage to a new lake. We were welcome to drag or carry the aluminum boats to the other lake as long as we returned them. We'd all asked how heavy the boats were, and dismissed any thoughts of portaging when we found out.

Still, I'd been back behind the cabin and I'd found the start of the trailhead, but it was obvious that it hadn't been maintained very much in the last couple of years. Finding myself with a few hours to kill, a feat that happened to us more and more, I set off with my knife and a daypack with two bottles of water. Finding the first marker was easy. Somebody had used a bright eye, basically a thumb tack with a bright reflective surface pushed into the bark of a tree. Using that as a starting point I walked down the trail, looking for another one.

I didn't see it, so I turned and found the tree that had the first markings on it and tied an orange plastic ribbon on it. It was marking ribbon; cheap and weighed almost nothing. I always kept a roll in my day pack for reasons just like this. A good way to get unlost if you find a string of ribbon. It'll lead you to a blind, or lead you out of the woods. In this way, I was going to give myself breadcrumbs to find as I returned.

"Wish there was more light in here," I grumbled.

The leaves hadn't turned yet, but they would soon. Once they dropped, it wouldn't be long until the snow fell. I walked in a semicircle and stopped when I found what looked like a mark hacked out of the bark of a tree. I stopped and turned, finding the orange ribbon about twenty feet behind me. I freshened the mark on the woods bark, exposing the lighter colored wood, and hung an orange ribbon on the tree branch above my head and then looked.

A small game trail had led between the two markers, but small brush and deadfall had obscured the trail. The small animals had made new trails to avoid the new obstacles, taking the path of least resistance. I couldn't do that since the trail led to a specific location, so I set out again, in the general direction that lined up with the first two markers. The third one I almost missed; the tree that had been marked had broken in the middle and fallen. A wind storm or something had snapped the top of the tree off. I almost didn't even look at it, but when I couldn't find a mark I'd started circling until I saw it.

Another stringer of marking tape and I had a pretty good direction to follow. With three markers, each roughly twenty feet apart, I could anticipate. After the dead fall, things got considerably easier and I kept hacking new marks, freshening signs on the bark of trees and hanging ribbon at eye level. I was surprised because I had lost track of time, but the trail opened up to a sandy beach about twenty feet deep. What startled me even more was the beached canoe and the nude woman washing her hair.

I stopped dead in my tracks, wondering where Tracy had found a canoe until she ducked her head under the water and ran her hands through it. She rose, pushing the water out of her eyes and I realized a few things all at once.

Number one, it wasn't Tracy. This woman was much younger and a lot curvier. I tried not to stare but it was difficult. Her blonde/red tinged hair looked almost brown as she squeezed water out of it when she noticed me.

With a yelp, she dove into the water up to her chin.

"I'm sorry," I said, turning furious shades of red. "I uh…"

"Turn around!" she yelled, her voice a bit lower than I had expected. "Who the hell are you?"

I turned around, the image of her nude form burned into the backs of my closed eyes.

"Tom Carter," I said, not yelling.

I could hear the water splash behind me and then footsteps. Something rattled in the aluminum boat and then she spoke up again.

"I've got a towel now."

I turned, and she'd wrapped a towel around the lower half of her body, a bikini top covering her chest.

"I'm sorry about that, I didn't know there was… are you… do you know what's going on?" I asked, confused and flustered and…

"I don't know what's going on, but when that Charter pilot makes it back here he's a dead man!"

"You guys are up here on a fly-in trip?" I asked, trying not to stare as she pulled the second towel from the canoe and began drying her hair.

She was definitely younger than Tracy, if I had to guess, she was in her mid-twenties. Freckles sprinkled across her face, chest and shoulders. She tossed the towel into the boat and pulled out a brush and roughly combed her hair out.

"Yeah," I'm Denise, Denise Wood. Do you know what's going on?" she asked me. "Because they were supposed to pick us up a while back and now our supplies are running low."

"Nice to meet you, Denise. Wait, you said 'our' supplies; there's more of you up here?" I asked her, shocked.

"Yeah, about an hour that way," she pointed behind her towards some woods, "What do you know?"

"Our pilot had just dropped me off when he

circled and crashed into the water," I said, sitting down putting the canoe on my right shoulder. "He survived the crash and told us that he saw a big flash and then his chest hurt. He died and we couldn't bring him back. He... We buried him. His chest, he had... a pacemaker. It had burned out because of the flash. All of my electronics are dead too... I think we were hit by an EMP."

I winced and waited for disbelief to wash over her features but she kneeled down in front of me. Eyes on her face, I scolded myself and was shocked when she sat in front of me, our knees touching.

"You're sure it's an EMP and not a CME?" she asked.

CME is Coronal Mass Ejection, a natural effect of solar storms from the sun. They can vary in intensity. The Carrington event in the 1800s had telegraph wires smoking and burning in some places. If something that strong were to happen today, it'd have the same effects as the EMP but I thought probably the Northern Lights we'd seen every night would have been brighter, and different... and no flash of light high up in the atmosphere. Also – why does a lady know the difference and how does...?

My heart thudded hard in my chest and I nodded.

"Pretty sure. Since our first day in, we've been prepping for the winter. I figured on paying a fine if I was wrong. I think they were supposed to have picked us up a week or week and a half ago?"

"I kept telling my mom and dad we should be getting ready, but Noooooooooooooooo," she said drawing out the word comically, "I'm just a crazy republican who should be wearing a tinfoil hat, and my little sister is driving me fucking bat-shit."

"Wait, you're a prepper?" I asked her, stunned.

"I do have a tinfoil hat somewhere, but since you came upon me all unaware while I was nude," I flushed at that, "I hadn't had a chance to get it on my head straight. What's it to you?" she asked, standing.

"I've never met any prepper ladies your age," I said, standing as well.

"My age? You think I'm ancient or something?" she asked and I let out a surprised bark of a laugh.

"No, I think you're mid-twenties tops," I said. "Most prepper ladies I've met are all in their forties and above."

"You're not too far off, Tom Carter. It sounds like you have family or friends up here with you, too. Any chance one of them is a doctor?"

Doctor?

"What's wrong?" I asked, suddenly worried.

"My dad has a pain in his lower stomach. He's had it for a couple days now, and today it hurt enough he didn't want to stand up straight when he got up."

"My buddy Jordan is an EMT, he knows some stuff; we could go get him?" I offered.

"Through there?" she asked, pointing to the woods behind me.

"Yeah. There's a trail between the two lakes… It hasn't been maintained so I was sorta exploring…"

"Yeah, me too, and finding a spot where my

sister won't drive me crazy. Still, can we go talk to Jordan?"

"Sure."

"Good. Can I come along, or do you want me to stay...?"

Let me think about that for a second...

"You're welcome to come along," I said offering her my hand.

She smiled at me and shook her head before turning and grabbing a pair of boots out of the canoe.

"I didn't bring clothes with me except the boots, in case the shore was rocky. Your wife won't mind, will she?"

"Ex-wife," I said, "and I think she won't mind one bit," I said, turning so she wouldn't see me smile.

"Ex-wife?"

"It's complicated...."

Jordan and Brian were stacking wood as I came off the trail. They were singing the banana boat song with Tracy's voice somewhere in the cabin singing "daaaaaaaaaaaaaaayyyyyyyyyyyyyyyy-oooooooooooo". We'd left a lot behind in the last two weeks. Privacy, modesty and pride. Group camp songs started out as a joke but they hadn't really caught on... but now...

The song trailed off as Brian noticed me first

and then Denise. She nervously put a hand on my shoulder and stood a little behind me watching. Jordan looked up and his voice trailed off into nothing and his jaw dropped open.

"Six-foot, seven-foot, eight foot bunch," Tracy sang as she walked out of the cabin with some trimmed ends of reeds to dump in the fire.

Her voice faltered as well.

"Hey guys, this is Denise. Jordan, her father is sick, she thinks he might have something serious going on."

"What… how?"

"The other lake, I found the old trail," I explained.

"Hi," Denise said, giving a small half wave with her right hand.

I caught the motion out of my peripheral vision, but I could tell from her voice she was nervous.

"Denise, that's Brian, Jordan, and Tracy," I said.

"Your ex-wife?" she asked.

"Yeah," I told her softly and Tracy looked at me, her eyes narrowing.

"Don't forget to check your boots tomorrow morning," I told her. "Jordan," I said turning to him, "Do you think you can help?"

"Yeah, I think so. Can I borrow some of your supplies?" he asked.

"Sure. What are you thinking?"

"Nothing yet, come on, let's get it. Denise, is it? What's your father's symptoms?"

Denise's left hand left my shoulder and she walked towards Jordan then into the cabin with him. I started to follow but Tracy stopped me up short, a finger raised to me.

"I...." I began.

"Only you," Tracy hissed.

"Only him what?" Brian asked, amusement in his voice.

"Only he could walk into the woods and find a swimsuit model," Tracy hissed and turned and walked towards the door of the cabin.

"Wow," Brian said. "She's right, though. What happened?"

I told him about finding the trail and being surprised to find a bathing Denise.

"So if all of us carried the boat, we could probably get that and the motor to the other lake in a hurry," I said.

"You think it's that bad?" he asked.

"I don't think Jordan was asking about my surgical kit, I think he was talking my medicine bag. The pain in the lower stomach, here," I said pointing it out, "sounds like something I've heard of. It's too high for the gall bladder, but she didn't say he was feeling nauseated... and to me, that leaves— "

"The appendix?" Brian supplied.

"Yeah," I whispered as the rest of the group came out of the cabin.

Not only did Jordan have my surgical kit, he also had my medicine bag as well.

"Want to take the—"

"Yeah, get our boat. Everyone grab a corner," Jordan said, his expression grim.

CHAPTER 9

The wind pushed our hair backward as I guided the boat into the wind. The little five horse pusher didn't leave a huge wake, not with five of us in the boat, but it did push us three times as fast as a person canoeing. Denise sat on the bench in front of me, directing me. Jordan sat next to her and Brian and Tracy had the front of the boat, watching for rocks or submerged tree limbs. I'd marked the trail head on this side of the lake with a dozen long orange stringers of marking tape, so going back would still be a pain but we could find the trail again, even in the dark.

"What's the worst case scenario if it is his appendix?" Denise asked.

"If it is, and it bursts, it would be really bad," Jordan told her – and it was all he would say on it.

NORTHERN LIGHTS

The sound of the motor carried much further than I must have thought, because by the time I saw the dock and the rough cabin, three figures were standing on the end of the dock. The largest figure had a hand over his eyes to cut down the glare, but even from a distance I could see he was standing stooped over a bit.

"My dad shouldn't be out," Denise grumbled.

I agreed, he didn't look well, even though it was probably a good thing that he was able to be up and about.

"What in the Sam Hell do you think..."

The man's words were cut off as I idled the motor down and everyone cursed as the boat suddenly slowed and our small wake pushed us forward, raising our bow slightly.

"Daddy, it's ok," Denise said, grabbing the edge of the dock and pulling a rope down from the cleat to tie off ours.

"Where did you guys come from?" the older woman, probably Denise's mother by the look of it, asked us.

"The other lake," I answered.

"He found a trail between the two when I was out exploring," Denise said, not mentioning that she had been bathing.

I was grateful for that because the looks I was getting from the three on the dock looked like they were ready to murder me.

"So it's normal for your company to just leave guests stranded out at the lake? What were you thinking?!" the man raged.

"Daddy, they're on a fly-in trip, just like us," Denise said.

Strangely, the third figure on the dock was a young woman. She was more slender than Denise and had blonde hair. There was no doubt the family resemblance, so it must be her sister. What struck me as strange though was the way her eyes followed the conversation. Never once did she speak, but more than once she gave me a strange look and then looked at Denise who was now talking to her parents.

"This is my father Daniel Wood, my mother Debra, and my sister Tonya. Guys, this is Jordan, Brian, Tracy, and Tom," she said, pointing everyone out and making introductions.

"You're stuck up here just like us?" Denise's mother asked.

"Yes, ma'am," Jordan said. "When your daughter asked one of us to come and help Mr. Wood, I offered to come. I'm an EMT back in America, so I know quite a bit…"

"But you're not a real doctor," Daniel said, disgust in his voice.

"No, sir. An Emergency Medical Technician. Most of my job is stabilizing a patient enough for a doctor or surgeon to take care of the problem," he said, leaving any hint of sarcasm out of his voice.

"So what do you know?" Mr. Wood asked.

"Your daughter described your symptoms to me; it's possible you're having an appendicitis attack," Jordan answered.

"That's something easy," Denise said, looking

back to me as we all got off the boat and onto the end of the crowded dock.

I looked around uneasily as it shifted under the combined weight of eight of us. The old wood posts were sunk into the lake's bottom somewhere, and they looked old. I was getting nervous when Mrs. Wood asked us to come ashore. Mr. Wood, on the other hand, grouched and bitched the entire thirty feet it took to get there. Tonya… never said a word, but her expression made me think she wanted to.

"But you're not a real doctor," Mr. Wood shouted from ahead of me.

"Your dad doesn't seem like he wants any help," I told Denise, who'd hung back to walk beside me.

"He hates doctors, he's terrified of getting sick. He's the healthiest guy I've ever known. He won't even take aspirin for headaches," Denise said, "That's why it worried me when he mentioned he felt lousy enough to see a doctor."

"Wow, it must be pretty bad," I agreed.

"Is Jordan a good guy? I mean, does he know his stuff?"

I knew why she was asking and, although I'd never seen him in action personally, I'd heard enough about his job from him and the exploits that sometimes made the newspaper. He'd fought off a PCP addict who had gone crazy after an OD, and then brought him back after he coded… Someone in a restaurant collapsed and he'd had to puncture the guy's chest to release air pressure that had built up, causing him to be unable to breathe, and done an emergency tracheotomy when somebody was dying from an allergic reaction they didn't know they had…

"Honestly, I brought the surgical kit with me on this trip," I started, "not because I know how to use it, but in the case it was needed, Jordan would have it," I said. "I hope we won't need it."

"See, it doesn't even hurt anymore. I can stand up straight!" Daniel's voice boomed.

Mr. and Mrs. Wood had moved away from the dock and were at a picnic table where Jordan had been poking at Mr. Wood's stomach area with a gloved hand. Denise looked behind her and smiled at her father's antics. She caught the eyes of Tonya who motioned something with her hands. Her fingers flew, and her hands made different shapes and motions. It dawned on me that she was signing. I'd never learned sign language so I didn't know what she was saying. I was even more surprised when Denise grinned and signed back.

"Your sister is deaf?" I asked.

"Yeah, since birth. She says my father's being a baby," she smirked.

"Maybe. This is a lot to take in, and frankly, I'm kinda shocked he even let us ashore. They don't know us and we showed up unannounced with their daughter and a boatload of strangers…"

"Yeah, well, after my antics in college I'm sure he's seen it all," Denise told me without looking and kept signing to her sister who was grinning ear to ear.

"Tom," Jordan yelled, "Bring the bag, would you?"

NORTHERN LIGHTS

"Got it," I said and reached in and got the kits out.

We'd stashed them in one of the plastic baggies in case the boat tipped, a wave splashed or it started to rain. Instead, I was carrying it by the top of the plastic and I stepped off the end of the dock and onto shore. Tonya gave me a once over look and then signed and I handed the bag to Jordan, before backing off a respectable distance.

"What do you think?" Tracy whispered, stepping up next to me.

"I was talking to Denise," I said. "But it seems like her dad doesn't want much help…"

"Not the dad, dumbass," Tracy hissed, "the daughter."

I looked back and Denise smiled at me and shot me a questioning look before turning away and signing. Tracy's head rolled back and she let out a hoarse laugh that brought everyone's attention to her. She let it out, holding her stomach and then wiped at her eyes. She cupped two hands in front of her chest and made a motion with them and laughed loudly again.

"Which one?" Both Brian and I asked.

"You're officially a dumbass," Tracy said and walked towards the picnic table to see what she could do.

"Why do I feel like I'm missing something here?" I asked Brian.

"Because you are a man," Brian said loudly.

Jordan looked up, watching us all for a minute, a smile on his face, and then he opened the medicine bag and pulled out a blister pack of what looked like condoms. They weren't, they were Azithromycin. A strong antibiotic I'd purchased through a straw man in Thailand, who'd mailed me what I wanted. Over there, you don't need a prescription for antibiotics, just money. There was a thriving black market that existed for preppers buying all kinds of medication because a lot of it was legit, if it was for your pet.

I know that sounds hokey, but it's true. Veterinary medicine, in many cases, is the exact same as human medications. It's not regulated the same way and you can actually get many different varieties at about 1/3 of the retail price if you were to have a script from your doctor and were paying cash for it.

"Somebody clue me in first," I said.

"Yes, if your appendix burst you will need these," Jordan said loudly. "The toxic shock might kill you."

"You can't be sure I had an attack or it burst!" Mr. Wood shouted.

"It's preventative since you won't let me look," Jordan shot back.

"You're not even a doctor, I'm not going to let you cut me open. There're no hospitals around here…" Mr. Wood's voice rang out again despite Mrs. Wood trying to shush him.

"What about the food?" Tracy asked me suddenly.

"I know, we'll have to go back soon either way," I said, "otherwise it'll spoil."

"I know, we don't have to drag the boat all the way back to the cabin right away," Brian said.

NORTHERN LIGHTS

"It's not like we need it for fishing," I told them both.

"When you guys go, can you give me a lift back, so I can get the canoe?" Denise asked.

I noticed her hands were at her side and she had a slight smile on her face. Tonya was a little red in the cheeks as well.

"Listen, Mr. Wood, if you don't want the medicine, it's better off with us. I'm not going to waste it on somebody who won't take it," Jordan said angrily.

We all turned to look. Mr. Wood was red in the face and Jordan was throwing his hands up in the air, before starting to pack the two bags.

"Listen to him, Dan," Debra was saying "It won't hurt anything to take the medication, just in case."

"That's what all doctors say, and then BOOM you're dead, or they give out vaccinations that make the kids autistic or deaf…" he looked over at Tonya who met her father's gaze and then deliberately stuck her tongue out at him and turned to face us.

She started signing and I could tell she was saying something serious to her sister.

"She wants to know if you can ask your friend Jordan to stay? We have an extra bedroom at the cabin."

"Why? He doesn't look like he wants to stay," I said nodding towards Jordan.

It was true; he looked pissed, Mr. Wood looked pissed, and the only one who was trying to smile was Mrs. Wood who kept touching her husband's arm or shoulder. Every time she did his volume went down and he calmed slightly, but he looked like a kettle that was fixing to boil over.

"Because I'm worried. I can bring him back in the canoe in the morning."

"I'll ask him," I said, "Just…"

"Ok, I'll take the damned pills!" Daniel shouted to his wife who just smiled bigger and patted his arm.

"Did Jordan just talk him into it?" I asked, confused by the sudden shift.

"It's whatever my mom whispered to him," Denise said. She's pretty good about it. My family's just kinda crazy… especially about health problems."

"How so?" I asked.

"My sis was born deaf, mom is diabetic—"

I winced at that, and Denise caught the look.

"So my parents are both on opposite ends of the scale on medicine and doctors."

"I'm sorry," I said, knowing it was more about her mom than her situation.

"Mom already knows. She's been out of medicine for about three days now."

"I've got books, I can go through them, see if there're any natural remedies," I told her.

"I've got some too," she said, "meet me tomorrow with Jordan and we'll compare notes."

"If he'll come," Tracy piped up.

"Oh trust me," Denise said looking right at her sister, "I think my sister can talk him into staying."

Tracy batted her eyelashes at us innocently. It took me a second and I snickered when I realized what she was saying nonverbally.

NORTHERN LIGHTS

"Jordan," I hollered, drawing his attention.

"Yeah?" He asked.

"Can you stick around here tonight in case there's a medical issue? The girls will bring you back in the morning?"

"Dude…" Jordan said loudly.

Tonya walked up, pulled a notebook out of her pants pocket and a pen from another and wrote out a quick note, handing it to Jordan. The look of annoyance faded from his features and he looked at me and nodded.

"Tom, tell me they have beer?"

I busted up laughing, and then Brian, Tracy, Denise and I said quick goodbyes. We planned to take Denise back to the canoe and then meet up there in the morning again.

"So did you just pimp your sister out to keep Jordan there to watch your father?" Tracy asked, a hint of snark and bitch evident in her voice.

"No, why would you ask that?" Denise asked from the bench in front of me.

"The way she looked at you when you asked for Jordan to stay…"

Brian busted up laughing and ended up moving from the seat next to his wife into the middle of the hull between benches. He was laughing so hard that I expected him to start pounding the bottom and the sides of the boat with his hands and feet.

"What's so funny?!" Tracy screamed.

"Oh God, it was a little bit of that, but it wasn't Denise trying to pimp out her sister. More like the other way around. Tonya was trying to get her sister and Tom…"

"What?" Denise asked, staring holes into Brian who missed the death rays shooting from her eyes.

"What, you think you two are the only ones who know ASL?" he howled.

"Clue a brother in man," I said as Denise's ears turned red.

"You know sign language?" Denise asked him, cutting me off.

"Yeah, and I caught almost all of it," Brian said, pounding on the sides of the boat.

"What was it?" Tracy asked, curious.

"Please don't," Denise pleaded, "At least wait until I'm off the boat."

"I can't hold this one out on my bud, but I'll wait till you're off the boat and we're into the woods before I tell him."

"I'm sitting right here," I complained, frustrated.

"Yeah, what's the big deal?" Tracy complained.

"I can't, it's just…" he howled with laughter, and it only intensified in volume the redder Denise's face became.

"This is embarrassing. I'm sorry about my buddy, he can be an asshole." I said trying to say something to ease her discomfort.

"He can be something, that's for sure," Denise said turning to face me.

"So what's your story?" she asked. "Tracy back

there is obviously the ex-wife, and your buddy married her?"

Tracy's ears perked up and she moved across her husband's writhing form and got on the bench seat next to Denise.

"What's wrong with that?" Tracy asked, an eyebrow arching menacingly.

"Isn't that against man law or something?"

That surprised me and I busted up laughing as well. They didn't notice it, but I also twisted the throttle a little more. We'd gone to their cabin against the wind, but for the return journey it was at our backs and I was opening the little motor up for all it was worth.

"It would have been," I explained, "Except I met Brian about six or seven years ago. What I didn't know, was that Tracy and he had gotten married. In fact, I kinda hoped that Tracy had been hit by a Mack truck or died in a train derailment... or maybe an escaped hippo ate her like the parents in James and the Giant Peach or—"

"That's nice, real mature," Tracy interrupted.

"You two are something else," Denise said, cracking a smile.

"You have no idea," Brian said, getting up from his spot in the middle and sitting on the front bench seat again.

"Shut up," both Tracy and I echoed.

I grinned, Tracy grinned, but Brian and Denise frowned. Someday he'd have to clue me in.

"Looks like we're here, that was a fast turn-around," Denise said as I cut the motor and let the boat coast into the sand, beaching itself.

"Yes. What time tomorrow?" I asked her.

"Don't have a working clock or watch. How about an hour after sun-up?"

"That sounds good to me," I told them.

"Thanks," Denise said and moved from our boat to the canoe.

"Have a safe trip back," I called.

"Thanks, you guys too. Thanks for helping. We really appreciate it." Tracy said.

"Bye," all of us but Brian chorused.

What was up with that? Was he feeling self-conscious because of me and Tracy having a ditto moment? That happened from time to time. Instead, Brian went to the front of the canoe and gently pushed it off the sand, giving her a quick escape to the open water.

"Hey, Denise…" Brian hollered before she got too far out.

"Yeah?" she called.

"Jordan knows sign language, too."

The cursing that came out of that woman's mouth left us all grinning, despite the foul language, and it didn't let up until we lost sight of her.

"Ready to get home so we can switch out that fish?" I asked.

"You just want to know what she said," Brian teased.

"Yup. That too," I acknowledged.

"Well, good. You should wonder."

"So are you going to tell him?" Tracy asked.

"Nope. Not till his revenge fantasy on you is

lifted."

"What?" I almost shouted, "That wasn't the deal."

"My deal was with the girl, not with you," Brian said.

"You're dead to me," I pointed to him and walked faster.

"You ever wonder why he's so anxious to find out what she said?" Brian asked his wife.

"Probably because he was checking her out," Tracy answered.

That stopped me dead, but they went on like I wasn't there, walking and talking.

"She was checking him out as well. Was telling her sister all about staking her claim since there weren't likely to be any handsome men left in this part of Canada, and she was lucky enough to flash her boobs right off the bat…"

"She did what?" Tracy asked, pushing Brian away from her for a moment.

"Tom walked up on her when she was taking a bath in the lake. 'Admiring the view' as she put it."

"The pervert," Tracy said.

"Yeah, said he was about as red as red could be when she saw him."

"Guys, I'm still standing right here," I said.

"So the sister wasn't being pimped out for Jordan to stay."

"Oh no, Tonya had her own ideas for Jordan; the two were gossiping like girls probably gossip all over the world since their parents weren't watching them. Seems they felt like they were going to die all alone and Tonya was telling her big sis to take one for the team…"

"She didn't look like she was complaining too much," Tracy said, now a little snide sounding.

"Nope. I think she was disappointed that Tom didn't have to convince Jordan harder."

"Still standing right here," I said.

Tracy turned back to look at me without breaking stride, "You can be quiet. Grownups are talking."

"Unbelievable."

CHAPTER 10

I was the first one up, and I visited the outhouse and then used some of the last of the hand sanitizer before heading to the campfire ring. I stirred the coals and added a couple of big chunks. The smoker had gone mostly out, so while that wood was catching I dug out the ash from the previous day and took it to the fish cleaning station and spread it around. I wasn't sure, but I thought it might help mask the smell and keep the bears from sniffing out anything that might fall from when we cleaned the fish. As it was, we used buckets of water from the lake to hose the top off.

So far, the bears had left us alone since our first encounter.

"You're up early," Tracy said, exiting the cabin and pulling the door shut behind her softly.

"Couldn't sleep much," I admitted. "Brian still out cold?"

"Yeah," she said, looking out across the lake.

There was a covering of fog or mist that rose up from the lake in the morning. The air was cooler than the water, making a light fog that burned away as soon as the sun rose fully, but it was quiet and serene. Sometime during the night it must have rained, because the grass was heavy with moisture and the bottoms of my pants were wet from walking about doing my morning chores.

"You need a hand with anything?" she asked me.

"No," I said, feeling hollowed out.

I'm normally a pretty happy go lucky guy, but there're days where I wake up and I'm just down. I mean, down in the dumps and can't pick myself back up. It had happened again and I had no idea why. It happened from time to time; no reason, no excuse. Usually watching football or hanging out with my buddies would alleviate it, but not quite cure it. Tracy knew what those days were like, and she did what she always did. She stood next to me and…

"Penny for your thoughts?" she asked. "Thinking about Denise?"

"No," I told her truthfully. "My mind is in a freewheel," I said.

"The thinking about nothing but brooding about everything?" she asked.

"Yes, pretty much," I told her.

"Anything in particular bothering you?" she

said, bumping her hip against mine, testing my balance playfully.

"Your breath," I said straight-faced and then dodged as she tried to push me. She almost tripped, but I caught her from going over and I laughed.

Just that moment, the sun rose on the far horizon and my mood immediately started lifting. I could feel the dark brooding thoughts burning away, just like the fog over the lake's surface.

"You're an ass," Tracy told me, but she was smiling.

"Yeah. What do you want for breakfast?" I asked.

We'd taken to cooking whenever we could on the bottom two shelves of the smoker to conserve wood, and, if we were going to bake something, that'd be the place to do it.

"Can you save some coals for me to try out a pancake mix?" she asked.

"Sure…" I said, curious.

She went back into the cabin, and a moment later came back out. She'd prepared the batter apparently, and it was in a plastic pitcher. I could see some crushed blueberries in the thick mixture and I smiled. She didn't know how much pucker power they had. Apparently she saw me smirking, though.

"I used some sugar to compensate for the sour. Now, get me a good spot in the campfire, this will only take a few minutes. I think."

I pushed the coals more or less even on one side and she set the cast iron pan down on the coals. Soon it was hot and I could see the heat rising off it. I watched as she used a thick towel to grab the handle and place it on the rack we'd scavenged from the Coleman smoker, and she put both over the fire where I was burning some larger pieces into hot coals.

"You look like you've been practicing," I told her. "I mean, you were kinda legendary for burning water."

That elicited an icy glare. "You can't burn water, asshole."

"Well, if anybody could, it's you," I said smiling. "Really, your cooking has improved."

"I took some classes and Brian's mother taught me some things," she admitted after a few minutes.

"Well, if those berries aren't too tart, this should be awesome!"

She poured the batter into the hot skillet and immediately saw bubbles rise in the batter. She pulled a plastic spatula from her back pocket where she'd hidden it and flipped it.

"Go get me some plates," she murmured.

I obliged and headed into the cabin where a shirtless Brian stood stretching, his hair a total mess.

"Where's Tracy?" he asked as I was walking out the door with three plates.

"Cooking pancakes," I told him.

"God help us all," he murmured, making the sign of the cross.

"You married her," I sniped.

"You married her first."

He was right, and my heart really wasn't into a

snark fest, so I pushed the door open and headed out. I held out a plate and she deftly flipped a pancake the size of the pan onto it. I set the other two plates down on the picnic table and headed back to the cabin. Brian met me at the door and I handed it to him. He already had the silverware in his hand, so I followed him to where he sat by the picnic table. I sat down and grinned.

"You didn't spit on it, did you?" he asked.

"Nope, but not a bad idea. Without syrup it might need a little something-something."

"You're gross," Tracy piped up, flipping the next one over.

I watched entranced as Brian contemplated his plate. He cut off a wedge and quickly stuffed a piece in his mouth, chewing furiously.

"Well?" Tracy asked.

Brian didn't say anything, instead, he held up a finger to finish chewing. He took another bite. I waited for him to fall over in convulsions, dead of instant food poisoning.

"It's different. Is this the cattail flour mix?" he said.

"In part, yes," Tracy said. "Mixed with some regular flour. Is it horrible?"

"It's not bad, it's just different than I expected. The blueberries were a nice touch."

My eyebrows shot up. Tracy flipped another pancake onto a plate and pushed it in front of me before turning to pour the rest of the batter into the skillet. I gave it an ugly look and then looked up to see both of them staring at me expectantly.

"What?" I asked aloud.

"What are you waiting for?" Tracy asked me.

"Your husband to fall over, kicking and screaming, holding his stomach and calling for Mommy."

"You're almost 40 years old, and you haven't matured a day past the ninth grade," Tracy said.

"Eigth, that was the best year of my life," I said, smiling broadly.

"You really should try it," Brain said, chewing another bite.

"You want mine?" I asked Brian.

"Why do you always rag on my cooking?" Tracy asked.

"Because you could never cook without burning anything." I told her.

She stood up straight, cocked her hip to one side and rested the hand with the spatula on it and pointed with her free hand. I'd wound her up enough to let loose with a verbal equivalent of a spear of vileness but I just smiled suddenly and took a bite.

"Now I wish I did do something to the batter," she muttered and watched me chew it.

It wasn't that the flavor was off, it was actually kind of good tasting... it was just a different mouth-feel and the texture wasn't the same light fluffiness I was expecting from my Waffle House experiences of years past.

"It's pretty good. Texture's different. Did you use baking powder?" I asked her, wondering if that's what was off.

"No, I wanted to see if it would make a big difference. The starch powder was finer than the regular flour so I wasn't sure if I needed it or not. And there's a lot more cattail flour than the baking powder anyways."

"It's not bad," I admitted, "I was expecting to die of…"

I grabbed my throat and choking sounds came out. Her eyes got huge. This had been the first time we'd tried the starch replacement. Falling off my seat and into the dirt, my legs kicked as I continued to make choking, gasping sounds. Right up until Tracy kicked me in the ass and I sat up grinning.

"You're an asshole," she said pointing at me.

"I know, it's one of my finer qualities," I said, quoting Jack Nicholson.

She finished cooking her own pancake and plopped it on the plate. I snickered when the one side was half burned. I must have distracted her too much and she didn't flip the first side fast enough, or the oil she'd used on the pan had absorbed or burned off. Either way, it only made me grin more and Brian kicked my foot right before I mentioned it aloud and snickered.

"They said an hour after sunup?" Brian said, trying to take my mind off of revenge and picking on his wife.

"Yeah. I figure that Betty Crocker here started cooking right about sunup, so when we finish breakfast and walk to the edge, it should be about time."

"Betty Crocker?" Tracy asked, picking up the spatula.

The better to hit me with?

"Ok, ok, Aunt Jemima?" I asked.

"You're digging the hole deeper," Brian said.

"I'll shut up now," I said and flinched when Tracy started swinging the spatula only to stop about a foot away from my shoulder.

"Don't let her hold a knife today, mmmmmmmmmmkay?" I asked Brian.

"No promises," but he was smiling and she was. too.

Maybe holding onto that hatred for so long blinded me to the fact that we could be more than ex's. I'd gone from a very uncomfortable hatred, only tempered by Brian's friendship, to actually getting along and teasing her. Life was really way too short, and I'd come a long way in both body and mind in the last few weeks.

"Jordan will have eaten there, I'm assuming?" Tracy asked.

"I wouldn't use the word assume," I told her, "but I am pretty sure they are going to feed him."

"Ok. The old man didn't really seem like he wanted Jordan's help, though." Brian told me.

"I know, I still don't quite get it, but he looked pretty old school."

"Yeah, a bit older than I would have expected. He was probably in his mid-forties when he started having kids," Tracy told me.

"I didn't quite mean it like that, but yeah. There's probably a huge generational gap there and having Jordan around, he probably thought he was a snake oil salesman."

NORTHERN LIGHTS

"It's not like they have anything we want to con them out of," Brian said.

"How about the daughters trying to pimp each other out?" Tracy teased.

"You never told me what she actually said," I told them.

"He's not going to," Tracy said with a sniff, put her nose in the air theatrically and headed down the trail.

"Why wouldn't they be here?" I asked.

"Nobody has a watch, man," Brian said looking out across the water.

The boat hadn't moved much; we'd beached it high up on the sand and thrown the anchor line around a tree a couple times just in case, but it had moved. I wondered if the wind picked up on this lake more than the one we were camped out at.

"Is it that simple?" Tracy asked, "Or should we just go out there and see?"

She had a point.

"We only have one more big can of gas," I pointed out, "but with as little as we use the boat…"

"It'll probably go bad before we use it up," Brian said.

"Yeah."

"Unless Jordan and Tom start visiting their new lady friends," Tracy said.

"I don't… wait, what?" I asked flustered.

"Let's push it in the water," Brian said changing

the subject.

I'll be honest, her words were a bit of a shock to me because I'd done almost zero dating in any recent history. In fact, there was only one serious girlfriend between Tracy and the present time. Lots of ladies went out with me on a date or two. Either I or they figured out that we weren't compatible or one of us would start talking politics and storm out of the restaurant, bar, whatever.

"You want to drive?" I asked them.

"Naw, you're the DD on this trip, why break tradition?" Tracy said with a grin.

"Great. Wonderful."

The boat launched easily, and when Brian used the oar to pull us towards deeper water by pushing off the bottom, I pulled the starting cord and played with the throttle until the little motor hummed. I put it in gear and we headed out. I'd love to say I remembered the way there perfectly, but I guess I'd spent more time checking out Denise than I thought on the way there because Brian pointed out a direction I wasn't headed in. I turned the way he pointed and was rewarded with the sight of the Wood's dock a few moments later. The canoe was tied up to one side, which I took to be a bad sign.

"Good thing we came, you think?" Brian asked.

"They're probably cannibals or the sisters have Jordan tied up in some sort of macabre, perverted and twisted—"

"Ok already, you're going to tell me what they said someday?" I interrupted Tracy.

They had talked about it last night, just quiet

enough to piss me off and neither of them would tell me what was said.

"Still no, you'll have to ask Denise," Tracy said making a shushing motion with her finger over her lips.

"Slow down, would ya?" Brian asked.

With a start, I realized that I had been going towards the dock too quickly. I throttled down and put the small motor in reverse and gave it some juice. It worked and we slowed down quickly, stopping next to a cleat on the other side from the canoe.

"Only ropes on the one side of the dock," Brian said.

"Use the anchor rope," I told him, cutting the motor and grabbing the back cleat with my hands, pulling the back of the boat tight with the left side.

We tied it off and stepped out onto the dock. We all walked towards the cabin and when we got close to the picnic table where Jordan had examined Mr. Wood the previous night, the door opened. Jordan stepped out, a grave expression on his face as he walked towards us.

"Hey, man, how are things?" I asked him, concerned because of his expression.

"It was his appendix," Jordan said. "It burst just before we got in yesterday. I had to open him up and clean out what I could." He flopped down on the picnic table.

"You ok?" Tracy asked him, sitting next to him.

Brian took the other side, but I stood there.

"Yeah, just tired. The infection will likely spread

throughout his body. I'm not sure that those z-packs are going to be enough, though," he said.

"How come?" I asked.

"Toxic shock to the system, his age, a ton of factors. He's already feverish. With Azithromycin you give two the first day, then one for like four more days. He's had two pills now, going on three. In 12 hours it should already be starting to work in his system. So far it isn't, and Tylenol and Ibuprofen aren't knocking back the fever."

"What's that mean?" Brian asked him.

"He's going into shock, and the infection will likely kill him. Even if I'd opened him up the moment we landed, it was too late."

The screen door of the cabin banged open and Denise and Tonya came out. Both looked like they'd been crying. Their eyes were red and Tonya's nose looked like it was rubbed raw. They took seats. There was extra room next to Denise and I ended up sitting after all.

"How is he?" I asked stupidly.

"He's hot, then cold. He's got the shivers," Denise told me.

Tonya started signing and Jordan and Denise signed back. Denise to me and said, "My sister said dad had the good luck to have a pervert like you checking me out from the lakeside and to tell you thank you." She said with a slight grin.

"Sorry about that," I muttered, and Jordan smiled wolfishly and began signing in a flurry.

I watched a second, amused slightly, but it was a somber moment and we were all trying not to think about the man who might be dying less than a hundred feet away.

"No," Jordan said, "I'm not going to tell him that," he was smiling and instead turned to me. "Tonya wants to know what you thought about what Brian had to say."

This time my face didn't burn so much as Denise's did.

"He wouldn't tell me," I admitted.

It was true, he talked about me in front of Tracy, but not to me. I had the gist of the idea but…

"Really?" Denise asked.

"Yeah, but I think he's got the main idea down," Tracy told her in a gentle voice.

That surprised me because yesterday and teasing me this morning I got the impression that she was being snippy/snarky and outright jealous when Brian wasn't around. Then again, every time I thought I understood what was going through a woman's head I usually turned out to be wrong. One day I'd have to write a book about it.

"Oh, well…"

An uncomfortable silence fell over the table. We sat like that for a while until something scared up two grouse near the water's edge, about a hundred yards from the dock. I watched them fly up from the tall grass and land down near the edge of the trees closer to the area carved out of the woods by the cabin's existence.

"It'll be some time till we know if it worked," Jordan said aloud to Denise.

"Daddy asked you to do the surgery; he must

have figured it out when he got sicker last night."

"I know. He was dead set against it until the shakes hit and the fever kicked in. Your buddy did a good job. The incision was barely three inches. Done in about two minutes."

"Oh God," I murmured, "what did you use for anesthetic?" I asked.

"Vodka," Jordan replied promptly. "Though the area was swollen and tender already. I think a lot of it was Mr. Wood just holding still and gritting his teeth. He's a stubborn but tough old man. You two girls don't lose hope."

Tonya started signing and Denise spoke, making her sister's words come alive, "I don't know what to do without my father. If somebody doesn't come soon, Mom will weaken and die because she doesn't have any more insulin. Were you able to find anything?" the last was asked as she turned towards me.

"I looked through my stuff. I remember seeing something about it, but I didn't bring that binder with me after all." I admitted, truly sorry.

"Thank you," Denise said, "from both of us."

Tears fell silently down her cheek and somebody kicked my foot under the table. I looked and met Brian's gaze. He never moved his head, but his eyes did. He looked at me and then flashed his glance over towards Denise. I got it, but I was waiting for the head motion. It didn't come, so I put my arm around Denise and pulled her close in a one armed hug.

She sobbed aloud for a moment. Tonya started

crying, seeing her sister let loose, and Jordan stood and wrapped both arms around her in a body hug. She allowed it and leaned back into him, letting him comfort her.

"You know," Denise said, rubbing her nose on her sleeve, "as a prepper I always thought the end of the world would be zombies and explosions. Not dying from lack of modern medicine and starvation."

"Nobody's dying," I told her, wanting to wipe the tears away.

Tracy leaned in on the other side of Denise and hugged her with her other arm.

"Not yet," Denise said to the group. "Without that medicine, I don't know how long my mom has. She's been on it for almost ten years now."

"We talked about this," Jordan said softly and paused when Tonya reached up and tugged on his arm. He sat back down and started again, so Tonya could see his lips. "We talked about this last night. We'll do all that we can for her. Make her comfortable."

I looked at him sharply. I could tell he already had a crush going on with Tonya, but I was more surprised by his offer of help. I knew he would do it just based on who he was and how I knew he'd react, but to hear it and see the grateful expressions on the girls' faces was still moving.

"Mom was already becoming insulin resistant," Denise told us, "so it's not like we're totally surprised, it's just that both of them—"

The screen door opened and Mrs. Wood walked

out, "Denise, dear, can you and your friends come help me a moment?"

"Yeah," Denise called back, standing and breaking my one armed hug.

We all stood as well and followed the ladies towards the cabin. The cabin itself was a newer log cabin, the wood still stained a golden color with cedar shake roofing. The porch was done up in rough-hewn pine, probably milled locally and stained to match. It was definitely a more lavish place than ours, but the outfitter who ran the lake the Wood's were at might have had more money or resources to build his cabin.

I ran my hands across the hand carved trim as I walked inside.

"The outfitter was going to have this as his summer home when he retired. Said it was the most remote cabin he had. I had no clue there was another cabin so close," Debora Wood said.

"Over the forest and through the woods," Denise sang out in a loud clear voice.

"We have a different outfitter," I told her. "They told me they used to run both lakes but sold off the rights to this one. I guess this one's supposed to have better walleye fishing."

"There's so many fish here, you could almost walk on the water," Mrs. Wood said and Denise wiped her eyes and cracked a smile.

"What can we give you a hand with mom?" Denise asked.

"If we're going to have guests, I want you to give me a hand with the cooking. I'm feeling a bit tired today."

That was an understatement. All of them, Jordan included, looked exhausted. I wondered if any of them had slept.

"Sure, what are we going to have?" she asked.

"See if you can scare us up some frogs. Your father liked them when you got him some the other week. Maybe he'll eat if you get him some more."

"He's not eating?" I asked.

"Last couple of days the pain was so bad, he said it made his stomach hurt. I'm worried if he doesn't…"

Mrs. Wood turned away and stared out at the lake.

"I'll help," I said.

"Tonya, will you ask your new friends if they can help you with bringing the wood closer to the cabin?"

Tonya signed back and her mother smiled, leaned over and kissed her on the forehead before making a shooing motion. I wondered if I was supposed to go with them or…

"Come on," Denise said, grabbing my hand and gently pulling me towards the front door,. "Unless you want to carry firewood."

"I'd rather catch frogs," with you, I almost added.

I knew the timing was wrong. I also knew I didn't know Denise at all, but she'd been kind to me so far. The fact that I was close to double her age had me hesitant, but by all indications, she was interested.

"You ever go frogging?"

"No," I admitted, "not on purpose."

"How'd you catch them by accident then?" she asked me as we walked towards the water.

"Usually trying to drop a hook through some thick lily pads to get at a bass or pike," I admitted.

"That's pretty much frogging unless you want to spear them or grab them with your hands."

"I'm not dressed for wading in the muck," I said, remembering that there were leeches in the swampy portions.

"Yeah, I don't like to do that either. We'll take the canoe. I've got two fishing poles in it already."

"Sounds good to me," I told her as she paused half a heartbeat to pick up a bucket that was next to the three steps going to the deck.

I followed her to the canoe. There was water in it, just like there had been in our boat from the rain the night before, but it wasn't much. A red solo cup floated near the back of the boat, where the person who steered sat.

"You want to drive or paddle?" she asked, giving me a look.

"I don't have to be behind the wheel. Ladies choose," I said blandly.

"Uh huh, not a control freak. I was wondering, seeing as you drove the boat both times yesterday from here."

"No, not a control freak. I think I got designated because Jordan hasn't used this one yet and Brian and Tracy don't care much to do anything, besides making my life hell and making out."

NORTHERN LIGHTS

"Old people make out?" Denise asked loudly.

I couldn't tell from her tone if she was joking or not. She knew the situation; I'd explained it. She couldn't be that dense, could she?

"Well, I don't obviously, but they do. I think to piss me—"

She busted up laughing, interrupting me. Just like that, she'd gone from somber to smiles and laughter. That said a lot for the kind of tension she must be feeling with both parents deathly sick.

"You like to be in the middle of these little… fits?" she asked.

"I don't know if I like it so much as I find myself involved in them somehow," I admitted.

"You bring it on yourself."

"That's possible," I admitted.

"Hm… you don't have to be right all the time. I like that. You can sit in the front, you'll paddle when we aren't cruising for frogs."

I got in smiling. At least I'd done something right. I untied the boat from the cleat and held onto the dock for her.

"What got you into prepping?" I asked her as she got in the back of the boat and undid her line.

I pushed us off.

"Where were you when 9/11 happened?" she asked me suddenly.

"I was at work, somebody announced it over the PA system and we all crowded over to the break room to watch the coverage on TV. Why, were you there?"

"No, but I was in New Orleans on August 23rd,

2005."

I let the date swish through my head a moment before it clicked. "Hurricane Katrina?" I asked, "You were there?"

"For the first two days," she said. "I left just as the police were going door to door, taking the guns from people."

"My God," I said pushing us off, "what was it like?"

Like many people, Katrina had showed Americans how ill-prepared we were for natural disasters and how ill-prepared people were in general. It was one thing to read about it or see it on TV. To have actually been there would have been horrifying.

"The first night, people were helping each other. I was visiting with friends from college and was stuck there with their family. We were lucky; their house was on one of the hills. The water hadn't reached it yet, but everyone else was camped right outside their doors. The morning of the 24th, a woman was raped and beaten on the cracked pavement in front of the house. We all hid inside and ignored people banging on the door for food and water."

"Did they try to get inside?" I asked her horrified.

"Oh yes, but with us being in one of the only spots where there was no water, the Red Cross came in quick as well and started ferrying people out. I don't think any of us slept that first night. The second night was eerie. Cops were banging on the doors of the houses, whether the steps were under water or not. I was shocked when some people answered. They were doing wellness checks and confiscating firearms."

"This story doesn't have a happy ending does it?" I asked her.

"I don't know if it's happy or not. We were there for two days, not the entire crisis…"

"Sorry, go on," I urged, paddling gently while she guided us down the shoreline away from the cabin.

"After the police had left, gangs of people would come and kick in the doors. There was gunfire, screams. Many people were leaving for the stadium. I heard it was even worse there."

"How'd you get out, then?" I asked her.

"A house three doors down from us was being broken into when the cops showed back up. We were evacuated north. We were lucky to get on a bus. Since I was there visiting, I just kept on going as soon as I got to an airport."

"That could have been a lot worse," I told her, "thankfully you got away ok."

"The woman who was raped didn't. The people who were beaten or killed by the thugs weren't. The cops… I don't know what to think about the people who shot and killed the cops and vice versa when they were trying to take their guns… I promised myself I'd never be in that situation again. I'd always be prepared for anything."

"And here we are," I said softly.

"Here we are," she agreed.

I turned around because we slowed and took

in her features. A sad smile stretched across her lips and she reached forward to pull a fishing pole out of the small frame that was holding it in place. She handed it to me. I smiled when I saw the stick bobber and the simple hook on the end. The most advanced tackle in the world couldn't out-fish a determined kid and a box full of worms with a rig like this.

"I'm sorry," I told her after taking the pole and getting the hook loose.

"For what?" she asked.

"I don't know, for a little bit of everything I guess," I admitted, "your parents, being stuck up here, what you had to go through."

"You want to know what really worried me this week? Even more so than being stuck up here?" she asked.

"What?" I asked her, not ready for the wallop I was about to get.

"Being stuck up here alone."

The words were simple, quietly delivered and they made me turn and meet her gaze. She held it for a moment and then her arm snaked out like lightning and hit the water. She pulled something out and threw it at me. Slime and algae was launched at me and I brushed at it frantically till it splashed in the water at my feet. She started cackling and almost tipped the boat as I leaned over and saw the bullfrog she'd snatched out of the water.

"That wasn't funny!" I said, half embarrassed, half amused and half angry.

I know, three halves... I was never good at

math, so sue me!

"It was," she said and went on laughing right up until…

I used the paddle and slapped the surface of the water on an angle and half the lake splashed up on her. Her laughter cut off in a gasp. I'd soaked her from about the waist up, her face and hair getting the brunt of the water.

"I hope you know how to swim," she said, standing.

My eyes opened wide and I quickly put the pole down and held onto the edges of the boat. She was going to throw me off, just like Tracy did…

She rolled the boat instead. I came up sputtering for air over her laughter.

"You wanted to play splash, let's play splash," she said, shoving a handful of water expertly at my head.

I blew the water out and wiped my eyes as I planted my legs in the squishy muck, pulling a lily pad off my face.

"You flipped the boat?!" I all but yelled, surprised and shocked.

"It all floats, even the rods," she said and sent another stream of water at me.

Two quick strides through the mush and she was squealing with laughter as I picked her up and threw her a few feet off into deeper water. I turned to follow, feeling something inside of me like butterflies right up until the moment that Denise didn't surface. Bubbles came up from the water but it was murky from our kicking up the muck. I ducked underwater, feeling for her when I felt the water surge behind me.

I rose up for air as two hands pushed down on my head dunking me. I got half a nose full of lake water and I tasted dirt. I spit it out as I surfaced again, two long sinewy arms wrapped around my head.

"I said catch frogs, not horse around," Debora Wood yelled from the porch of the cabin.

Immediately Denise let go and I turned to see her mother's form, both hands on her hips, scowling. Luckily, nothing had been lost to me, though if I didn't get out of the muck I might lose my shoes.

"Yes mother," Denise said, trying to sound chastised but when Denise turned to face me, her mother broke out into a smile.

"You're a brat," I told her, wading towards a paddle that was floating towards deep water.

"That's what I hear." she replied, sending a half-hearted splash my way.

CHAPTER 11

Thank you for staying for an early dinner, I know the girls and Jordan said you've all been busy," Mrs. Wood said.

"It's no problem, ma'am. It's nice to visit company," Brian said jovially.

He'd been ribbing me every chance he got when the Woods elders weren't around. Apparently the whole thing had been seen by everyone but Mr. Wood, who had finally fallen asleep. I wanted to say something snarky to Brian but just nodded in agreement instead.

We'd ended up dragging everything from the canoe to shore before we righted it and then emptied it of water. We'd caught easily three dozen frogs by hand or just by holding a hook just in front of their faces. They didn't even need a worm, just the small object and the swaying movement to convince the big croakers that it was a fly of some sort. Put them in the bucket, put a lid on it and keep fishing. Denise had showed me how to dispatch them by poking them in the head with a fillet knife before cutting off the back legs, then the webbed foot. We'd skinned the legs easily, battered them with a cornbread mixture, and pan fried.

"This is really good," I said with a mouthful.

"It'd be better if you didn't smell like sewage," Tracy told me.

"I went for a swim, so sue me," I told her grinning.

"Are you two related? Brother and sister by chance?" Debora asked.

I looked at who was fighting off the giggles and covered my mouth for half a second, wiping the smile away.

"No ma'am," I answered, "Just known each other since the sixth grade."

Brian's head jerked around to fix me in his gaze, "I didn't know that?"

"She was my neighbor. Her parents' moved in next door."

Brian looked conflicted, but instead of pushing it, he grabbed a couple more frog legs and started eating again.

"Is Mr. Wood awake?" Jordan asked. "I need to check on him again."

"He said to let him sleep till it was three, when you said he needed to take the next pill?"

"Yes," Jordan answered. "I just don't know…"

"Oh, I have a wind-up clock," she pointed to the stove where an old brass clock sat.

I looked at Brian and remembered our conversation from earlier and just nodded. He nodded back in understanding. I'd never thought about the wind-up clock, and it made perfect sense. I saw we had another twenty minutes until we had to wake him up.

"What are you doing for food over on your lake?" Denise asked me.

All eyes turned to stare at me. I swallowed my bite and told her.

"Fish, smoked and dehydrated. Cattail roots for the starch to make bread… Blueberries… and I brought a few dried goods, but they won't last us long."

"We've been eating mostly fish ourselves," Deborah translated for her daughter.

"I've got to learn how to sign," I said to myself, softly.

Apparently not softly enough.

"Oh, if you stick around long enough, the girls will teach you. They love to sign when I'm not looking; always getting into mischief, those two."

"I'm sure your daughters are proper ladies," Jordan said with a serious look.

Debora giggled at that and looked away.

"Or not," I answered smiling.

"What are you planning on eating meat wise? You can't just live on fish, not these ones anyways."

I knew she was right; there wasn't enough fat content. When we got back, I was really going to start my hunting and snaring efforts in full, even if it was just for some steaks in the short term.

"Moose, elk, bear," I told her. "By the way, do you have any bear nearby?"

"No, why?" she asked.

"We've got a mother and two almost yearlings by us. Gave us a scare." I told them.

"No bear problems, but we don't leave any food out," Debora said in a reproachful tone.

Apparently she'd been on trips like these before.

We talked about what we thought was going on, how we were preparing for the winter. Mrs. Wood was adamant that somebody was going to come and fly them out soon, so she hadn't seen the need to do more than plan the day-to-day food. Since frogs and fish were plentiful, she'd been safe from the ravages of hunger. So far. Denise let her arm rub my side and I looked over. She hadn't used her elbow but she was giving me a look. It took me a second, but I realized she was letting me know she wanted to talk later. I nodded and was startled when the old brass wind up clock started going off.

"That's the signal," Mrs. Wood said standing.

"Do you want some help?" Jordan said rising.

"No, you keep Tonya there entertained. I'm just going to fix him a plate and make him take that pill."

I grinned wolfishly at Jordan who was suddenly squirming with the attention of everybody still at the table. What? It was nice not to have it directed at me for once!

"Yes ma'am," he said and sat down.

Tonya hadn't missed much of the conversation, and I figured she was an expert in reading body language because she took his left hand as he sat and pulled herself closer to him and laid her head on his shoulder. He looked ready to bolt.

"Don't fight it, stud muffin," Tracy told him.

"What do you know?" Jordan said after thinking about it a moment too long.

"Well, my husband here knows ASL also, and he told me all the sordid details—"

"I thought you said you didn't tell him!" Denise said, cutting her off.

"He didn't tell Tom, but he keeps nothing from me," she said sweetly.

"That's right," Brian said in a weird voice and leaned over and kissed her.

Tonya made a motion pointing her finger down her throat and silently gagged. I nodded as the two sisters started signing. When they looked at Jordan, Denise made her finger and thumb hold themselves apart like they were going to make a giant pinching movement. Tonya shook her head and she brought her fingers closer together so they were only an inch apart.

"What's she saying?" I asked Brian who was trying not to laugh. "Telling her sister how big Jordan is?" I guessed.

Denise let out a surprised snort and turned to me. "No, I was asking her how much more it would take to embarrass you two boys. You're awfully shy.

It's kind cute. Funny to boot."

I looked to Brian questioningly, and he was nodding and making a fist and shaking it up and down. Jordan shrugged and went back to eating and soon we were all chatting again. Where we grew up, what we'd wanted to do after college. Silly stories, which Tracy knew the most about and made sure to make me the happy go lucky goofball in all of them instead of the brooding angry young man I'd actually been. Maybe she was helping me out, or maybe my perception had been off.

"I'm going to check on Mom," Denise said aloud, translating for our benefit.

Jordan signed something and she nodded. He rose and followed her.

"I wonder if your dad was able to finish the frog legs?" Tracy asked Denise.

"I hope so, he hasn't eaten much lately—"

"Denise!" a loud nasal-sounding voice yelled.

She immediately got to her feet and left the room.

"Who else is here?" I asked.

"I think that was Tonya," Brian told me, "some of the deaf folk don't always like talking. They know they sound a little different. Self-conscious," he said.

"How do you know so much about deaf culture?" Tracy asked, and I turned to hear the answer for myself.

"Same way that Jordan does. Family member. For me, it's a cousin. Jordan's little sister is deaf…"

I loud wail went up and we all rose to our feet and hurried towards the short hallway that separated the main dining room from the bathroom and two bedrooms. The yell had come from there. As we grew closer, I could hear soft sobs. I pushed open a half-closed door and, sitting on the bed, holding Mr. Wood's hand, was Debora. Tonya was kneeling near his other hand and Jordan and Denise were standing at the head of the bed. Jordan was checking for a pulse. I could already see the color had gone out of Mr. Wood and for a man who'd been sweating earlier, his brow was now dry.

"He's gone," Denise said and turned to sit by her mother.

"Oh God," I said, backing up, bumping into Tracy and Brian.

"Don't freak out," Tracy whispered to me, putting a reassuring hand on my shoulder, "it's ok, don't freak out."

"I…"

"He's cool, hun," Brian whispered.

"No, he's not."

Memories swirled. My parents and then grandparents. No siblings. Watching my father in a sickbed, every trip to visit him at the hospital he'd shed a few more pounds from his already gaunt frame, until one day I walked in and they were cleaning the room. The nurse had been trying to get ahold of me, but I'd left school to go visit my dad. It was the year I graduated, the year I left, the year I ended up marrying Tracy.

"I…"

Denise must have seen something because she rose and walked over, wrapping her arms around my chest and cried softly.

"What happened?" I asked her.

"When Mom came in here, he was gone. He went in his sleep."

"It was the infection," Debora said. "His body couldn't take it. He told me last night that he didn't think he'd…"

Tonya stood and pulled her mom off the bed and held her frail neck and head to her chest. Silent tears coursed down the deaf woman's face, but her expression was blank. She was trying to be strong for her mom.

"I love you, Mom," Tonya said aloud.

"I love you," her mother said.

I don't know if Tonya could hear something or feel the words through their contact, but she squeezed her mom tight and then let her go. Debora stood and looked at the four of us standing there.

"I don't know what to do," she said simply.

"Let's go sit down," Denise said, leaving me and walking towards her mother and sister. "Out in the dining room.

"I want to check—"

I nodded at Jordan and he shut up. He wanted to check the incision. I figured he'd never rest easy unless he assured himself that he didn't screw up, or hadn't done everything within his power. He was just built like that. It was both a good trait and a character flaw because, if he found something he did or didn't do that caused the death of Mr. Wood, he'd flog himself for it.

I felt Tracy's hand leave my shoulder and I

walked out of the room, and went out the door to the wooden deck and sat on the top step. I heard the door open a second later. When somebody sat down beside me I was expecting Tracy or Denise, not Brian.

"Dude, you ok?" Brian asked.

"I… Yeah," I said.

"What happened?" He asked simply.

"My father. Cancer, died in bed."

"How old were you," he asked.

"Eighteen, just a month away from graduating."

Brian was silent for a moment, probably mentally counting back the years.

"I'm sorry man, that kind of stuff hits you bad?" he asked.

"Yeah. My… I haven't been able to go to funerals," I admitted.

"I know this is going to sound like shit, but everybody dies someday, man."

"I know, it doesn't make it easy, though."

Brian leaned in, hitting my shoulder with his. "And quit making me look like a loser in front of my wife."

"What?" I asked, surprised.

I turned to face him and saw he was grinning. "Gotcha. Listen, I was uncomfortable earlier. Part of me was jealous I guess. You two have a shared history. I didn't realize it went as far back as sixth grade and a white picket fence separating you two."

"Yeah, we were friends first. Should have just stayed friends."

"You were young," he said.

"Young and stupid," I admitted, welcoming the change in subject. "Brian, I just want you to know, man… I've kinda had an epiphany up here…"

"If you try to kiss me I'm going to knock your teeth out," Brian said, making me chuckle despite the situation.

"I'm done trying to nurture my hurt feelings and anger towards Tracy. I'm done with that. I just hope you trust me, that I'd not break the friendship by…"

"Dude, I know. It looks like you'll have your hands full, though. You and Jordan both."

"I don't even know what to think about that," I told him, "I think what I'm feeling is mutual, but I've only known her a day."

"Sometimes that's how it works. Sometimes that's cupid shooting you in the ass and not the heart. Either way, just go slow."

"Her father just died and I'm too chicken to go in and be with her, trust me… I'll be lucky to even manage slow - if she'll even talk to me," I said dropping my head into my hands a moment, letting the afternoon sunshine on my head.

A headache was forming, and it was going to be a doozy if I didn't get in the dark somewhere soon.

"Just be there for her," he said getting up and walking away.

I heard the door shut and felt footsteps as somebody walked out and sat down next to me. Tracy? Wrong again. Denise sat so close our hips touched and leaned her head over on my shoulder. I put my arm out and around her.

NORTHERN LIGHTS

"What do we do?" she asked through the tears.

"We'll bury him," I told her. "We'll live on."

It really wasn't that simple was it?

"What about Mom? She hasn't got much time left."

"You won't be alone," I told her and she cried harder, her arms encircling my chest.

CHAPTER 12

Weeks later, we were back at Denise and Tonya's cabin, digging another grave. Debora's health had faded quickly once her husband was gone. It was a testament to how much she'd been putting on a show for him, so he wouldn't worry more than he already had. She'd got so weak she'd not leave the couch or bed for long periods, and she slept more and more. She quit breathing in her sleep and never started back up. The girls had waited a day to come by canoe and found us at our little homestead putting up more food.

They were no strangers to our site and Jordan and I had gone back and forth when we had free time, as did they, but they'd never left together before. I took one look at their expressions and went and got Jordan. That's how we found ourselves under the same tree that Debora had picked out for her husband. The shoveling was surprisingly easy, and when it was done, we placed her to rest beside her husband. Carving her name in the tree below her husband's was our last act.

Both canoes were loaded with what remained of their clothing and supplies and we towed them back to our side of the lake. I didn't tell them that they'd left a treasure trove behind, but it was too soon and it would be ghoulish of me to even suggest it.

"...and you can totally have my bunk," Jordan was telling Tonya.

I was only hearing part of the conversation. He wasn't signing to her, but speaking aloud. It was how nervous he was. Unlike me and Brian, he'd never really slowed down long enough to notice the ladies or get attachments. He had fallen and hard. I knew I really liked Denise, but it wasn't the bone crushing, all encompassing—

"Penny for your thoughts?" Denise asked and my hand slipped off the throttle, making the boat lurch wildly.

I righted it and apologized.

"What was that?" she asked.

"Tracy says that. A lot. Just threw me hearing you say it," I admitted.

Tracy smirked from her spot at the front of the boat next to Brian.

"I was thinking about everything. I wish we could do more; I wish…"

"Look at that," Jordan interrupted, and I looked

to where he was pointing. Swimming across the girls' lake was a moose or an elk. I never figured out which was what and was too embarrassed to ask.

"Doesn't even care that we're in a boat, zipping across the water."

"Nothing changes up here for them," Brian said. "Boats and planes came and went. I wonder how long it is until not even that's going to happen."

That thought was a lot darker than what I'd been thinking and we all fell silent.

"Have you set out any snares like you were talking about?" Denise asked, probably to break the uneasy silence.

"Yeah, I've got about a dozen small to medium sized game sets out. I'm going to make a deer snare later on today, actually."

"What if a bear or elk steps into it?" Jordan asked.

"Should hold. I'm going to use the cable from the aircraft. Some of that is 3000lb weight strands. That big coil is made up of a ton of strands. We just have to see if I have stoppers and stuff to make them."

"Yeah, you sort of forgot about that," Tracy snarked from the front. "Like you were going to do that a couple weeks ago."

"I know," I said.

Other than putting up food and firewood, we'd done very little else. Each day, a pair of people – for safety – went and collected the now ripe blueberries, enough to fill two or three of the screen window trays that we'd made. We ate as much as we dried, and craving the sweet juices had us all wondering about fermenting. That was something that Denise had hinted at she knew about. In all, we'd see. It had also gotten colder in the last couple weeks and we'd been wearing our sweaters in all but the heat of the mid-day sun. Summer was coming to a close, and soon Fall would take over.

"We don't have to bring it all at once," Denise told me as I cut the motor and beached the boat on the sandy beach on our side.

"It isn't a big deal," I told her. "It's the boats that might get left just on the trail somewhere."

"I don't want to be a bother; we still haven't figured out the sleeping arrangements as it is."

Tracy smiled and started to say something as she was stepping off the boat, but her husband clamped a hand over her mouth and whispered something into her ear. She nodded and grabbed a big backpack full of Denise's gear and headed off. We'd all done the trail so much, it was clear and marked out on both sides of the trees to make it easy for everyone to navigate. We grabbed the contents of the boat and went back to our little homestead.

"So, what's for dinner?" I asked aloud.

"Your night for cooking. Just pick something non-toxic," Brian said.

"Ok, so I'll leave your wife's cookbook out of it," I said. "Who's in the mood for some biscuits and rabbit stew?"

"Rabbit stew?" Tracy stopped and turned around to look at me.

I pointed. The snare I'd set on a lark a couple

days ago to show them how I did it was now sprung. It hadn't been when we'd left to go bury Mrs. Wood, but it looked like a nice fat cottontail.

"Damn, just that easy?" Jordan asked.

"Sometimes," I said walking over and untying the rope I'd used as an anchor line and slung the carcass over my shoulder.

"You know how to clean them?" Denise asked me.

"Of course, do you?" I asked her, curious.

"I love rabbit," she said, and Tonya made a face at her.

Denise stuck her tongue back out at her sister and we got walking again. I know, for grownups, we sure acted maturely. Then again, we were in the middle of nowhere, with almost no entertainment. Snark, sarcasm, and pranks had become the new norm, although campfire songs were still highly rated.

"What do you have for veggies?" she asked.

I didn't.

"Nothing really," I admitted.

"Ok, I've got some stuff in my pack. Rabbit stew it is." Denise walked faster, leaving me the last one in the line of friends.

"Ok, so you got a big piece of cable. This is so entertaining," Tracy droned in a monotone voice.

"You're not helping," I told her.

"You wasted some of your weight on that? That

has to be like, 8 pounds."

"Something like that," I told Jordan.

"What is it?" Denise translated for me.

"It's a crimper for my snare parts. Now, this isn't the usual wire I use, it's stiffer and is slightly different dimension,s but it's close enough for me to crimp parts with it."

"This is like the rabbit snare you had earlier then?" Brian asked.

"It will be. The only difference between that one and this one," I said drinking a cup full of the thick stew, "is the weight of the wire and the type of cam lock I use."

"Ok, so break it down for me," Jordan said leaning in close.

We were all sitting around the kitchen table and I was having mock snare class while we ate.

"You put in the cam locks on the unprimed wire. Go ahead and let it fall to the bottom for now," I said heading off Tracy's questions she was already trying to ask, "Then loop the end, cam locks open end, making a loop. Then crimp on a stop ferrule." I paused to show them.

"Put a double ferrule on one end and push it in three inches roughly. Then take the end that's sticking all the way through, and make a bend and guide it into the open hole," I told them as I showed them.

I finished the crude loop by crimping it closed with my tool that looked like bolt cutters.

"That's it?" Tracy asked. Just a basic loop.

"Hold your arm out," I said and when she did, I pulled it tight.

Jordan took a hold of the wire and pulled, testing it, "And they can't back out?"

"No, they have to mess with the cam locks to do it. If we were snaring monkeys I might worry, but we're not," I said smiling.

"Well, show this monkey how to release the cable," he said grinning. I showed him.

"Then you take the small loop and use that to attach it to a tree or a drag."

"What's the drag for?" Jordan asked, "Why not just hook it to a big tree?"

"Depends on the placement and what you're likely to snare. For something low to the ground like a wild boar, I'd say tying off to a tree is ok. Going after something bigger like a bear or an elk... I'd probably prefer to use a drag."

"Ok, but what is it?" Tracy asked.

"A log or large rock you can tie the snare off to."

"Why, though?"

"Well, you want the animal to get its air choked off and die as quickly as possible. Sometimes something big like a bear can just push a tree over and get loose if the loop didn't close tight," I told her. She nodded.

"And you know this illegal method of taking deer because..." Denise asked, an eyebrow arched in a question.

"I watch a lot of YouTube," I said going for a chuckle but it fell silent and dead in front of us.

"Sorry, no more YouTube. My bad," I apologized.

"Hey man, at least somebody here knows," Jordan said.

"Now you do, too. Placement is something you're going to just have to get a feel for, that and picking out how to set up the traps for whatever it is you're hunting."

"How long you been doing this?" Jordan translated for Tonya.

"Since I was a kid," I said shrugging.

"Why are we just now getting real meat then, huh?" Brian asked, adopting a high pitched voice that got him an elbow to the gut by Tracy.

"That's for stealing my line," she said and then leaned in to give him a kiss.

"We've had so much going on," I said, "I dunno. I think putting back as much as we can at this point would be the smart thing to do."

"Hey, we could always go see what's in the old cabin by us sometime," Denise piped up.

"What do you mean?" I asked, surprised.

"There's an old cabin further back in the woods. I think it's the owner's original. The roof's still on, but it's in rough shape.

I looked around and everybody shrugged.

"It's worth a look sometime," I said, thinking about the sheets that had been left behind for lack of room, all the million billion little things they could use.

"Ok, so now that I've had some real meat, I want MOAR!" Tracy yelled in her imitation of Brian's bass voice.

I smiled and noticed that Tonya was nodding and making that knocking motion with her fist.

That must mean yes.

"Good, so I have a ton of traps to walk tonight, and then we'll figure out the sleep situation."

"Yeah, about that," Tracy said slyly.

"Don't," I pointed at her.

"What?"

"You're dead to me," I said and she picked up part of the biscuit she'd had left on her side and chucked it at me.

"What was that for?" I asked her, finding the chunk that landed back on the table and eating it.

"You're stealing my lines now too!" she pretended to pout but was smiling.

Tonya signed and when she was done both Jordan and Brian snickered. Denise smiled.

"What?" Tracy asked.

"She says that someday when she grows up, she wants to be a sassy spoiled brat just like you."

Tonya's mouth dropped open and she quickly signed, looking at her sister.

"Apparently we weren't supposed to tell you that, she was joking of course."

"Of course," Tracy said pointing two fingers towards her eyes and then using them to point at Tonya's.

"I'm watching you."

"It's getting deep in here," I said, slurping down the last of the stew, "I'm going to go check my traps. Anybody want to come with me?"

Surprisingly, it was Tonya who popped up with her hand raised high up in the air.

"I was going to go for a walk with him," Denise

said, arching a curious eyebrow at her little sister.

"You were going to show me how to use your necklace spark thing for making a fire," Tracy whined.

I shrugged and Denise gave me a smile and shrugged back.

Tonya walked beside me. Whenever I could, I tried to turn my head to her when I talked so she could read my lips. I showed her the simple game trail sets I'd set up on a game run. She smiled and we kept walking and checking them. One of the hoops of the snare was partially closed and Tonya looked at me questioningly and then held the snare off the ground a little bit as if to ask me what happened?

"I think a squirrel or something pulled it down. They like shiny stuff sometimes."

She nodded and we kept walking after I made that loop larger. I was setting things for really small game. Rabbits, raccoons. Nothing like squirrels or birds, though I wouldn't turn one away if I got it. Which reminded me, I took my day pack off and pulled out the AR-7 Old Henry camp gun and put it together. Tonya stopped to look at it, fascinated.

"You ever shoot?" I asked her.

She nodded. I put it together and handed it to her.

"That's the safety on it, and this is how you re-lease the magazine," I showed her, "and this is the charging bolt..."

She smiled and pulled the bolt back, feeding a shell into the chamber.

"We don't want to scare the animals off," I told her, thinking she was going to take a potshot at something.

Instead, she held it up as if to aim at something, dropped it down and put it back up getting the feel of it. For somebody who didn't like to speak even though she could, she made herself known through body language and basic hand gestures. I didn't have to understand sign language to see now that she was just checking out the gun.

She held it up and pointed to the safety showing me it was on and then handed me the gun.

"You shoot one like this before?" I asked her.

She shook her head no and then held her hands out almost 3' apart and then held her hand out in front of her body making a big circle with her thumb and pointer finger.

"A bigger rifle or shotgun?" I asked her.

She nodded, smiling and then tilted her head to the side, telling me to come on, hurry up.

"So can I ask you something?" I asked as I fell into step beside her.

She nodded.

"Why don't you talk? I know you can."

She was quiet for a long time and then spoke, her voice monotone and a bit nasal sounding.

"My voice sounds funny to other people. Embarrassing."

"Well, it's just the six of us up here," I told her. "I don't think it's funny sounding."

She smiled and clapped me on the shoulder. I

pointed up ahead and her eyes followed mine to the last of the snare sets. It was almost all the way to the blueberries. This one was also empty. Like the one before, something had pulled on the loop a bit, or I didn't set it up right.

"Let me," Tonya said.

"Ok, sure," I said watching as she went and made the loop larger again.

She studied it for a moment when she was done and then looked at me and held up a finger.

"Wait," was what she told me and then went and collected dead sticks. She shoved them into the ground on either side of the trail. I watched halfway fascinated as she made a tunnel of wooden sticks. It would channel an animal right to the snare if they went that way. Would the sticks spook them?

"Bait?"she asked.

"Bait? I don't know what to use for bait." I said.

"Grass? Berries?"

"Ahh yeah, there's some of that, and it's close by."

"I follow," she told me.

Brian had told me about that one night. That ASL doesn't always have a direct translation into English. There are a lot of connecting words that are left out and context was conveyed with expression and body language. I understood her easily enough, and I wasn't about to make fun of her. I honestly didn't know anybody who would. There are plenty of assholes in the world, though.

"Let's go," I said bowing, with a mock flourish.

She smiled and we headed out towards the meadow.

BOYD CRAVEN

There we were, picking blueberries again. I leaned the camp gun on a tree next to what had become a stomped down row from previous pickings. I'd given Tonya a clear plastic food bag from the stash I always kept on me, and we were picking. She was eating about half of what she picked, saving the other half. I didn't know if her idea about baiting the snares with berries would work on anything more than a bird, but it was worth a try. I'd done a ton of experimenting as a kid and the only real cost to it was time.

I moved further up the hill and started picking in a spot I hadn't gone through before, turning around to check on Tonya from time to time. She kept smiling and giving me a thumbs up. They probably had been low on fresh fruit as well up there. I warned her about cramping her stomach up by eating the not quite ripe ones, but she was going to town, ripe or not. I moved to my right a bit and smelled something familiar. I moved my knee where I'd been kneeling. A small plant low to the ground had been the source of the scent.

The leaves of the plant made me hesitate, so I pulled out my knife and moved it in case it was poison ivy or something in the family. Instead, what I found were small white flower blossoms on some of the plant, with long runners and red berries. Strawberries to be exact. They were small, almost the size of a dime. I picked one and bit into it, seeing if it did something funny to my tongue. Nothing but

154

the awesome flavoring of strawberry jelly. I picked some and looked at the hillside in front of me.

The berry plants were everywhere. I wondered how we hadn't really noticed them… unless they were only just starting to fruit? I started going slower in my picking and mixed both berries together in the bag. Everybody was going to have a field day when they found out! I was turning around to get Tonya's attention to show her the strawberries when I heard a grunt and something large moving up the hill.

The mother bear without her cubs was loping up the hill of the berry meadow. The gun, where was the gun? I screamed for Tonya, waved my arms. The gun was down towards the front of the meadow, closer to Tonya and the mother bear than me.

"Tonya!" I screamed and started to run.

Running towards her, I dropped the bag of berries and worked on getting her attention, screaming to hopefully scare the bear and trying not to fall on my face. She still hadn't looked up. I was perhaps two seconds away when the bear sped up, its body covering more distance as it hung close to the ground.

At the last second, Tonya looked up, startled by me running and screaming as the bear clipped her side, sending her sprawling. Tonya hadn't been the target? Or was I the—

Our bodies collided. I was running downhill off balance to try to keep to my feet, but at the last moment, I lowered my shoulder like I would in football. When we hit, my world exploded in pain and

I went up and over the bear. It had been like hitting a charging rock, and all the breath left me. I landed on my back hard to see Tonya running towards the base of the hill. Good, she would get away.

The bear, on the other hand, was getting up, and it didn't look impressed. It hadn't landed on its back or had its breath knocked out of it, it'd been merely stopped. It rose on two legs and roared at me loudly before taking two steps and bringing its front paws down hard, on my stomach. I rolled into a ball, suddenly nauseous. I always read that if attacked by a bear, protect your vitals and play dead.

That didn't work.

I curled my knees up to my stomach and held my arms over my face but when the bear bit into my left shoulder I let out a blood-curdling scream of pain. One big paw smacked me in the head, I could feel the claws ripping into my flesh and like that I couldn't see in my left eye. The pain was huge and so terrible I didn't know how I was even conscious of it.

The teeth sunk deeper and the bear tried to pick me up by my upper arm and shoulder. When it couldn't, it started smacking and clawing at me. On my right hip was the knife, if I could get to it—

Claws and teeth tore into me, everywhere. All at once. I was blacking out and I couldn't help it. I heard a tiny, popping noise. It went off six or seven times. Maybe more. Then something heavy hit me and forced all the air out of my lungs, muffling my screams, muffling my breath.

Darkness.

CHAPTER 13

"Hey, there you are," somebody told me. Female voice.

I couldn't open my eyes or, if I could, I couldn't see anything. Every part of my body was wracked with pain from head to foot. My left hand was a throbbing mass of pain and even trying to flex the fingers left me gasping. What didn't hurt, though, was the warm wet feeling of somebody slowly washing my face.

I couldn't talk. The pain was too much. I worked on breathing.

"He must have stopped when he got across the border. He's got Tylenol 3s with codeine," I heard Jordan say.

I had stopped. Why wouldn't I? I didn't need a prescription there for it and it was the strongest pain killer I could buy. I couldn't say that, though; the pain was too intense. I felt a soft hand open my right palm up. Apparently my fist had been clenched and clenched tight. I felt the blood start to flow into the fingers as they started to tingle.

"Tom, listen, man, take these. I've got more stitching to do," I heard Jordan tell me and two pills were pressed to my lips.

I took them in, using my lips and tongue. A straw was put in the edge of my mouth and I took enough of a sip to swallow. It left me feeling breathless and the pain—

Muted light, voices. The pain was huge, but it wasn't as bad as it had been a day ago. Was it a day ago? A week?

"I don't know if you're awake," I heard Tonya's voice and felt a hand tousle my hair, "but you saved me. Thank you."

I felt a gentle kiss on the top of my head and I tried to move.

"Don't," I heard Tracy say, "you're going to give Denise and Tonya a complex if you get up and get hurt."

I tried to talk but my mouth was dry, my tongue sticking to my mouth. I knew my lips were cracked, but I imagined they'd had a hard time getting me to drink when I was awake. I coughed.

"Squeeze your right hand if you can hear me."

I squeezed and was surprised to feel a soft hand

squeeze back.

"Do you want a drink of broth?"

Oh yeah. Despite the pain, my stomach felt hollowed out and it had an ache of its own. I squeezed the hand. I felt whoever it was let go of my hand and then get up off the bunk. I managed to open my right eye and everything was a muted orange gauzy glow. I couldn't open my left eye; I could feel the heavy gauze padding over it now. It must be bandages that I was looking through. Even muted, the light hurt as if my whole body—

I felt a straw in my mouth and sipped. I was mostly awake. I could feel a pair of rough hands working on the bandages, probably dressing them. Whenever somebody had pressed pills to my mouth I'd taken them, I'd lost track of how many times it had happened but it'd been a few. I opened my eyes.

This time it was both, and I could see out of both. My left eyelid felt funny, gummy.

"Hello," I said after I sipped a good amount of water.

"Hey, you're back."

"Feel like I got run over by a Mack truck," I said, my throat so dry the words made me cough.

I tested my legs and found they worked easily enough but weren't in terrible pain. In fact, my shoulder and head were the worst of it, along with the dull aching thud of my heartbeat that I could feel in my temples.

"How long?" I asked.

"It's been three days," Denise said, kneeling down so I could see her face.

She sat Indian style in front of me. "We've all been taking turns taking care of you."

"What happened?" I asked, reaching my good right hand out towards a water bottle with a crinkle straw.

"Tonya never heard the bear coming. She said she saw you charging down the hill and then she was knocked to the side and you tackled the bear."

I cracked a smile, which made the side of my face hurt. I winced, and that made it hurt.

"Wasn't a tackle meant for the bear. Was trying to get her out of the way."

"Well, that's what we figured because you don't have 'crazy' or 'stupid' tattooed on you anywhere. Trust me, I looked."

That made me grin. If I'd been out for three days, somebody had to have been cleaning me up and taking care of me. Gross.

"So then what?" I asked.

I remembered part of the attack, curling up, teeth, pain.

"She said it kept pounding into you with its front paws and then started clawing and biting at you. She ran for the gun and was coming back as the bear was lifting you up by your shoulder and slamming you around. You'll have some nice scars."

"How bad is it?" I asked her.

"He almost scalped your forehead. He missed your nose but you got raked on the left side. It missed the eyeball but split the eyelash and scratched the eyelid. I thought you were scalped when Jordan and Brian brought you in."

"The bear?" I asked.

"My sister put the barrel of the gun to its ear and kept pulling the trigger. It fell on you and she couldn't move it, so she ran back here and got us. Nobody would let Tonya and me see how bad you were at first. I thought… I mean it was my fault. You were…"

"Am I going to live?" I asked her when her tears slowed.

"If you don't get an infection. It's a good thing you brought up antibiotics and that Tylenol 3. As it is, Jordan had to operate on your hand. The bear's tooth broke off when it bit through the bone. He had to get it out."

"I don't remember much."

"What were you thinking?!"

That was the big question. Had I been thinking anything? I was in terrible pain, but I had a beautiful woman sitting in front of me and I had just enough medicine in me to take off the edge so I didn't scream. What had I been thinking back then?

"I remember thinking that if I let something happen to your little sister that you would kill me," I answered her truthfully, "and I've already got one ex-wife up here…" I paused to take a sip of water. "And there'd be no way I'd survive with two angry women under one roof. I'd have to take my sleeping bag to the outhouse."

The words were meant to be truth and humor,

but her mouth pulled tight, her lips into a thin line. After a moment, she put her head down on the edge of the bed. I wanted to run my hands through her hair, but I was holding the water bottle. I was trying to find a place to sit it down when the door to the cabin opened, sending a brilliant flash of white light straight through my skull and making me wince in pain.

"Oh good. How are you doing?" Tracy asked.

"I feel like hammered shit," I told her.

"Can you walk?" she asked.

"Give me a hot meal, a shot of Jack Daniels and a month in a beach resort and I might be able to manage a wobble," I admitted.

I felt weak on top of the pain, but I didn't know if I could walk or not.

"Well, we have to get you up and move you, or you'll get bedsores. I am not helping with bedsores."

Denise got up and took the water bottle, putting it on the kitchen table, and joined Tracy at the edge of the bed. I moved my legs, but as soon as my ribs and stomach muscles tried to move, it was agony.

"Careful," I heard Tracy say and then she had my right arm over her shoulder.

Gently, taking me under my injured shoulder, Denise got under me and together they helped me get my balance and take the worst pressure off my torso as I stood.

"Did it," I said, sweating and swaying.

"I've rigged up something from my preps that you're going to love. It'll even make your soreness go away some," Denise said.

NORTHERN LIGHTS

Being this close to the girls, I could smell their hair; they both had recently been shampooed and none of it smelled like lake water. Curiosity made me wonder. With much fumbling cursing and resting, I made it out of the cabin to another four pole tarp wrapped contraption closer to the fish cleaning station than the smoker and dehydrators.

"What's that?" I asked, dreading the steps it would take to travel the thirty some odd feet to it.

"I made an outdoor shower. We've been waiting for you to be awake enough to get you in there. When the pain was too bad, you'd just pass out. Give you too much medicine, you slept. We started cutting the medicine back last night to see what kind of shape you were in," Denise said in a rush.

"Yeah, the shower thing... it's lovely," Tracy said smiling, running her hands through her hair.

"We fill a black solar shower bag from the filtered cistern water and then when it's warm we take a shower. We've been running buckets to the filter for the cistern for ages now to make sure it's topped off. I think we've got five gallons of hot water for you."

I tried to smile, but I did manage a grimace. It hurt my face too much otherwise.

"Ok, let's go," I said. "But I want Jordan or Brian around in case I fall down."

"Can't," Denise said with a shrug.

"Why is that?" I asked, smelling a rat.

"Jordan, my sister, and Brian took the boat and your lock pick gun to finish emptying out our cabin and the old shack. There's even a shed back there."

"Let's stop at the picnic table then," I told them after we took a couple steps, "and I'll wait for them."

"Listen," Tracy said, the snark out in full force, "it's not like we want to watch you bathe. You need to and you need to not fall on your ass. We have to make this quick because that bear meat is greasy and it's causing issues in the smoker. The whole damned thing is full, and we're about to have a bunch of meat go bad if we don't…"

"Ok, ok," I said, too tired to argue.

We made it to the shower enclosure. The stakes had been dug or driven into the ground and back-filled. They were lashed together with cross bracing that looked like nylon rope that made a web-like structure through the top which was open to the sky. A black water bag and a shower head coming out of the bottom awaited.

"There's no door," I said.

"Actually, we do have one like what you made for the smoker and dehydrator," Tracy said. "But you're not steady on your feet."

"But you're not…"

"Come on, Brian, it's nothing I haven't seen before. This isn't creepy; you need to clean up or you may get an infection."

"Denise?" I pleaded.

"I told you already and I agree, it isn't anything I haven't seen before either. Just let us help."

The wind picked that moment to blow and I shivered. I was wearing a cotton button up plaid shirt. One of half a dozen I packed. It hadn't been buttoned and as I worked my way into the 4' by 4' shower the shirt fell open. My entire torso and side from belly button to nipples was bruised.

"I only remember him stomping on me once," I said.

"When my sister shot him, he fell on top of you. I think it was the nerve endings firing off that kept the legs twitching for a minute. Or he got you more than you realized.

That was possible.

I reached up with my good hand and grabbed the rope support above me as the girls helped me strip down to my boxers.

"Those can stay on," I said.

"You've been in bed for three days. Trust me, you don't want those on." Tracy said.

I sighed and stepped out of them. Denise held onto me and Tracy reached across me and turned the shower valve till a steady stream of water fell. The first drops shocked me by how warm they were, and then it was just bliss. Hot water. I closed my eyes and let it run over my body and was about to wipe the water out of my eyes when Denise grabbed my left wrist.

"Can't get that hand wet yet," she said.

"How am I going to wash up with just one hand?" I asked, feeling a creeping sense of horror.

"Oh come on," Tracy said. "We've all seen each other naked. This isn't going to be weird." Which made it weird.

Ok, it wasn't weird, but it was a bit humiliating. Still, I put up with it and I found more places that hurt than I knew I had places. Still, the hot water slowly relaxed me and many parts of me that had been screaming in agony reduced their wails to a dull throb. Until the washcloth and soap was introduced. I endured that as well and was wrapping myself in a towel when I heard Brian call out.

"Hey Tracy, you're never going to believe what we found!"

I made sure the towel was pulled tight. The last thing I wanted to do was to walk around bare-assed in front of anybody else.

"Hold on, we're getting Tom dried off."

"Need a hand?" he asked.

"Yeah, just have Jordan and my sister take a quick walk," Denise shouted.

"Got it," Jordan said.

It wasn't long after Brian showed up and the four of us stumbled our way into the cabin. I was put on a chair near the table as Brian helped me get on a pair of boxers and sweat pants. When he was done the ladies turned around and went out to call for Jordan. With me awake and upright, they wanted him to check me out again.

"Dude, when we used to joke that you were all Davey Crocket with this prepper shit, I never thought you'd go and tackle a bear. Why didn't you have the gun on you?" he asked.

"Wasn't thinking," I told him, wincing in the pain as he looked me over.

The punctures on my shoulder were discolored from the iodine mixture I'd brought up and there were neat black stitches closing many of them off. They had angry red marks all around them, almost like bruising. Hell, it probably was bruising.

"Hey man, you bounced back fast," Jordan said walking in with the rest of the gang.

"I'm not back, I'm awake," I told him.

He checked me over from the waist up and had me move my left arm in a series of motions. That left me panting in pain… Then he checked out the gauze bandages over part of my face.

"You got those wet," he said.

"Yeah. How bad does it look?" I asked him.

"When the inflammation goes down it's going to leave a pretty nice scar. A good plastic surgeon can take care of it if… I mean… you dumb fuck, why did you go and tackle a bear?"

"I had three seconds to act and move. I don't know if there was much thinking involved," I told him, "other than not letting Tonya get hurt," I told him.

"I appreciate it by the way," he said, his voice softening. "It's a good thing you're a crazy prepper and your ex-wife is here."

"Oh, why's that?" I asked him.

"Because I didn't know you were allergic to penicillin and was about to give you a ton of it when you first got in. Luckily you had some other stuff in there too. Tracy recognized the name as the stuff you used back in the day."

"Yeah, I made sure I had stuff that'd work for any situation."

"I'm worried about your hand," he said peeling the rest of the gauze from my head and looking it over.

"How bad?" I asked.

"His tooth broke off in the bones of your hand. I've got it braced. Had to open the top of your hand up to get it out. If that gets really infected… I don't know if I have anything strong enough that you can take." He said quietly before starting to unwrap my hand.

"If I get really bad, I've got an epi pen, some Claritin, and Benadryl," I told him.

"I don't know what you mean," Jordan told me.

"They had to do that to me at the hospital once when I got into a car crash. They shot me full of epi and then gave me a liquid z pack."

"I've heard doctors do that, but I'm not trained… I mean I've never had to do it."

"If it comes to it, I've got the supplies, don't worry, man."

"What if your hand doesn't heal back up and it's crippled? What if we have to amputate it because I fucked up?"

"What if you suddenly grow boobs and start prancing about in high heels?"

Tonya let out a loud bark of laughter and soon the whole room was busting up. I even laughed because it was funny, it broke up the tension and there had been very little to have fun with.

"Now, between Denise and Tracy, they got something special cooked up. It should be ready soon," Brian said from the back.

"Tracy cooked it? Are you sure I have enough antibiotics in me, doc?" I asked.

"You want another hole in your head?" Tracy

snarked, but she was smiling.

"Yeah, he's going to be fine," Brian said and kissed her, shutting her up effectively.

"How are we doing for food and firewood?" I asked.

"Oh, you're never going to believe it!" Brian said, getting all excited.

"Yeah, it's some good news," Jordan said with a grin.

"What is it?" Denise, Tracy, and my voice chorused as one and then we broke out into smiles.

"Whoever the owner is was one smart guy. He had 2 metal 50-gallon drums in the old cabin. The circular lids were bolted closed. Bear proofing, I guess. Inside of one was extra hats and gloves, boots and a ton of those metal traps."

My heart raced with those words. Leg holds or conibears, it didn't matter to me. When a snare wouldn't do it, those would, and none of us had coats. Which made me ask, "Were there any coats?"

They shook their heads.

"Well, that sucked. What was in the other barrel?" I asked.

"Food, well, dried stuff. Flour, cornmeal, packets of yeast. Beans, rice and spices!" Jordan said the last like he was about to be served a four-course meal.

"Wow, he was planning on an expensive dinner date, wasn't he?" I asked sarcastically, but secretly I was happy for the food and those were the same staples that made up a good portion of my preppers pantry.

BOYD CRAVEN

"It was stuff that wouldn't go bad if it was frozen," Jordan said.

I thought about that. Maybe it was an old trappers cabin and it was the supplies one man would need for the winter. In theory, a 50-gallon drum would hold more than enough dried goods for a person for a season. The problem I saw was that there wasn't one, there was six.

"That's great news," I said.

"Now, what's the special dinner that's going to make me happy?"

"Bear Burgers," Tonya said smiling. "We brought the meat grinder from the cabin on our first trip. We've had the burgers on the lower rack on the smoker for an hour now. Low and slow, as long as it doesn't start another grease fire."

My mouth watered at that.

"Buns?" I asked.

"Well, they're more like oversized rolls, but yeah."

My mouth was watering. "Ketchup and mustard?"

"I have packets from McDonalds I found in my luggage. My just in case mom and dad didn't pack enough, and they didn't."

"A real feast," I said smiling broadly.

"Oh yeah, and we found some wild onions, so…"

"You're killing me," I said. "How didn't I smell this?"

"It's in the smoker for one, for two, you reeked of BO, medicated ointment and sweat. You were probably smelling yourself."

"So I smelled like Tracy's cooking?" I joked.

I was surprised when it was Tonya who came forward and got in my face. At least, she stood in front of me so she could see my lips clearly.

"You always pick on her. She helped my sister take care of you. Be nice." Tonya told me seriously, her voice soft despite the words and warning.

"Can't help it. It's been like that forever. I hope she knows I'm not being serious," I said turning to look at her.

"Most of the time I know you're not serious," she said. "I'm ok, though, Tonya. He isn't bugging me."

Tonya nodded and then turned, hugging me hard enough to make me hurt and then kissed me on the cheek.

"Thank you. I didn't want to be bear food."

"No problem, kid."

The smile made the scabs on the side of my face ache, but I couldn't help it. I thought of what it had been like for the three days I was out cold. They had all stuck by my side and taken care of me. I felt like we were even closer now than we had been if that was possible. I did feel horrible about the timing, though. The girls had just lost their mother and we'd just gotten them back to the cabin when this happened. They wouldn't have had much time to grieve.

"When do we eat?" I asked as everyone started moving away.

"Soon," Tracy is going to check on the burgers

and I'm going to finish patching you up and then give you more pain pills," Jordan told me.

"I'll just hang out. I can't help much," I said lifting my left hand up showing them the mitten of gauze it'd become.

"You're going to love this," Denise said and went out to help Tracy.

"How is the food situation when we add the trapper's supplies?" I asked Jordan.

"Some of the fish is starting to go bad. We'll have to keep an eye on it."

"I can't wait to try some burgers out," I told him, "I'm famished."

"We've got enough meat to have burgers for a week or more," Brian said, "and still have some bear jerky."

"Have you tried any of the meat yet?" I asked, curious.

Jordan and Brian looked at each other guiltily, but it was Tonya who spoke up, "We had it the next morning after you saved me. It was good. My sister found onions in woods by last trap."

"You're talking an awful lot," I told her.

She smiled, "You and Tracy are the deaf ones, not my fault you don't know sign."

I smiled at that and she wrapped her arms around Jordan, hugging him as he finished smearing triple antibiotic ointment on exposed stitches.

"I want those to air out. You ready for your hand?"

"No," I admitted.

I was wrong; I was ready, but I didn't know if I wanted to see it.

CHAPTER 14

As the weeks passed, we had to start a fire at night and one in the mornings. I was only confined to the inside for a few days, except to bathe, before I was steady enough on my feet. I think the problem had been lack of food and a touch of an infection, but it cleared up rather fast. We decided it was due to the magic of the bear burgers.

Never before had I had a burger that tasted as moist and as good. I didn't know if it was the smoke, or that we'd been living on almost fish and berries forever but it was amazing. Luckily, Denise had made the guys save the organ meat, and we all had small amounts of the liver, even though a couple of us – including me – didn't like it.

If we tried to live like this forever, we'd die of

starvation even if we had food, but we didn't. We had to survive just long enough. The other change was the bugs seemed to suddenly disappear. We didn't have to walk around with a fog of spray to beat back the mosquitos. Actually, we'd run out of that long before and had just barely tolerated the little buggers. It was amazing, but we were starting to layer our clothing.

The guys continued to gather firewood, and Tonya and Denise checked on the snares. Firewood became our biggest priority, that and making sure we had enough food.

"What are you doing today?" Denise asked, sitting down next to me at the picnic table.

"They found an old radio…"

"Yes?" she asked. "But the battery is dead. We could use the acid we found and fill it up with what water we have. It isn't distilled but…"

"We could," I agreed. "But would it work?" I asked.

"We could always go on a day trip together and go get it. I know they were really excited about finding the food and loaded all the boats up, but I think there's still stuff we could get before winter hits."

"Yeah, me too. I'm worried a bit. About the winter time, I mean."

"Do you know how much snow it gets up here?" she asked.

"No," I admitted, "I think we should go on that day trip though," I said standing.

"Really? Some alone time?" she asked, her hand finding itself in mine, our fingers intertwining.

"Yeah, if they have the acid mix there, maybe we can figure out how to tan the bear hide we smoked… and if we keep going on the other hides we've been getting…"

"We might have a coat or six?" she asked hopefully.

"I think we can figure out how to make one just from the bear fur. At least for you ladies."

"You know, I think you deserve that one," she said, leaning into me.

Her weight was soft against me. My ribs had been bruised but not broken; they were still tender but as we sat there watching the fire and the sunset, I didn't want to be anywhere else with anyone else.

"Maybe," I said one arm hugging her with my good arm.

My shoulder had healed up fine, and all the stitches were out. Still was some residual soreness in the shoulder. I'd watch for signs of infection.

"Tom?" I heard Jordan's voice call out.

"By the cabin," I hollered back.

"I need to borrow the gun; is it by you?" he asked.

"Yeah, why?"

I didn't control it like a monopoly, but we decided to keep it close to us where the food was. We'd seen one of the bear yearlings taking the fish offal where we dumped it. The second one we hadn't seen again. If somebody was going out that direction, they always took the gun, otherwise, it was here close to where we were preparing and cooking food.

"Remember that night you showed us how to make a big snare?" he asked, coming into view from the lakeside.

"Yeah?" I said my voice lowering as I could see him clearly, Tonya at his side.

"Well, we got an elk and I want to make sure it's really dead."

"How did he get in there with his horns?" I asked, curious.

"Girls don't have horns," Tonya said.

"You do," I said pointing my fingers at the sky and holding them next to my head.

"You better not call my sister the devil, you just like to pick on people," Denise said, mock tickling my side.

"I think we might need the boat for this one, though," he said.

"The gas motor?" I asked, hoping he said no.

"No, we can take the row boat. I think it'll be easier to quarter it and load it up."

"Keep the hide intact," I said.

"You got a crazy idea, don't you?" Jordan said grinning.

"I don't know how to sew, though, and tanning the hide is going to be… interesting."

"I thought we didn't have the stuff to do that?" Jordan asked.

Denise started signing and Tonya and Jordan smiled and nodded, making the yes motion with their hand. I knew that much, and some basic words but Denise was sitting beside me, not facing me and I wasn't used to looking at it that way.

"What?" I asked.

"Do you want to make our day trip an over-night trip? We'll pack sleeping bags."

"Ooooooooohhhhhhhhhhhhhhh lala," Tracy drawled coming up behind us. "A romantic get-away."

"You're not funny," I told her.

"Actually, she is; look, he's blushing," Brian said walking up.

"Don't you guys have some firewood to split?" I snarked.

"Naw, this is more fun."

"Great," I said with a big sigh.

"I mean, you don't have to if you don't want to," Denise said, but she appeared to be enjoying my discomfort.

It was sometime in October, maybe later if I could remember properly. I was just worried about the trip through the woods. I hadn't traveled fur-ther than to the dock since the bear mauled me.

"I do," I told her softly.

I meant it.

It felt good to be on the water, the wind and spray hitting me in the face. Even though it was starting to get chilly, I really loved it. A muskrat or a beaver popped his head up near a shoreline and then went back under the water as it caught sight of us. The four of my new family had left us to go square away the elk and we'd packed lightly for the trip. We had

177

enough dried food to make a decent meal.

"You know, a bottle of wine, a little cheese and some of that smoked cured bear meat would go good right about now," I told Denise who was sitting on the seat in front of me to be close enough to talk but not so close that the boat was unbalanced.

"I've got an idea about the wine," she said, grinning, "You might even like it."

"You know how to make wine?" I asked her.

"Yes, Dad was big into brewing beer, but I always liked wine better. We have blueberries not grapes, but I think it'll be the same. Don't have the right kind of yeast, though."

"I'm not sure how long those blocks of yeast are good for," I admitted.

"Hey, even if it turns into vinegar, it'll be worth it. It's a win-win."

"Just don't forget why we're here," Denise said with a grin.

"For the radio and the battery acid," I said deliberately being oblivious.

"I'm not zipping my sleeping bag up with yours now," Denise said with a mock pout.

"Sure you are unless we make a fire in the cabin. We have to share body heat," I said grinning wolfishly.

We'd shared a kiss once. There was a lot of baggage that neither of us wanted to talk about, but the trip would give us the space to. The fact that I had such a long history with Tracy, how I couldn't quit poking fun at everyone. The fact I'd almost gotten her sister hurt... and my being a healing mess. I knew I wasn't looking very pretty. I'd gotten a good look at my reflection on more than one occasion. The fact that Denise still wanted to be near me was surprising to me. The fact she wanted an overnight so we could be alone… terrified me.

I had no problems with sex or ladies in general. No hang-ups. I was worried that it would change the dynamic, but my body wasn't worried. It wanted her with a need so primal I could barely hold still sitting near her some days. I didn't know if girls feel the same way when they are attracted to somebody, but Denise put every girl out of my mind when she was near.

"Do you think that radio will work?" she asked.

"It sounds like a really old radio. They said they really didn't dig through that stuff much, figuring it was fried like everything else."

"What if it's an old shortwave set?" Denise mused.

"We could call for help," I said softly, the motor barely making a noise. "Or at least, find out what's going on in the world."

I heard something. I killed the motor just as Denise was going to say something and tried to isolate the noise.

"Behind you," she said.

I turned to look and saw a glorious sight. It was a large jet. It had come in from the East. It would see us, if the flare…

"Oh shit," I said, burying my face in my hands.

"What?" Denise asked.

"They're all taking care of that elk. Nobody is at

the cabin where the flare gun is!" I told her.

"There's nothing we can do," she said, "I wonder who it is?"

"It's a jet, so it isn't necessarily looking—"

"Look!" Denise screamed.

A bright red flare flew straight up. It was well ahead of the jet. We watched it race up into the air.

"I wonder how visible that is from the air looking down?" I said aloud, suddenly wanting to cry with sheer joy.

I didn't know who was back at the cabin, or why, but they were there and almost immediately got a flare up into the air. We had four rounds for it and the directions, but more than two shots would start to melt the barrel of the orange plastic gun.

"I hope so. Look, the jet is altering course!"

We watched for close to ten minutes. The jet made a slow lazy circle between the two lakes. Another flare shot off into the air and the jet rocked its wings left to right and then straightened out after one more rotation and left the area.

"Do you want to head back?" I asked her.

"No, let's go ahead and have our night. They won't be back today," she said.

The way the sun was setting and the way the light reflected off her eyes caught me off guard. I moved forward to the middle bench beside her, kissing her deeply as the northern lights started coming out to light up the night sky.

CHAPTER 15

The sun wasn't up, but we already had the boats loaded. We were towing back one of the canoes packed full of the rest of the supplies we'd found at the old cabin. I'd not tried the old radio yet, but I'd found the alligator clips to hook it up to the small lawn mower battery we'd found in one of the metal drums. The other thing that had me excited was the traps.

Sure, we were probably going to be rescued, but I'd let somebody else worry about returning the supplies. If, for some reason, it took more than a few days, I'd start putting out the traps and life would be normal. Well, as normal as it ever was going to be. I worried what being rescued might mean for Denise and me.

I hadn't been looking for a relationship, and

I really didn't have one, but in another way I did. Since I met her, I'd felt this connection with her and yes, there was a comical first meeting, but that meeting had turned into friendship and then it had deepened into much more. I don't exactly know when it happened. It seemed rather fast but, in fact, we'd been together for every day since their mother died, and I was fond of her from the first day, so it was even further back than that.

The thought of being rescued was both exhilarating and terrifying. It was all we'd talked about as we shared the sleeping bags at the trapper's cabin after we'd made love... but what about after we were rescued? I mean, would she want to stay with me, or go back to her old life? None of us knew what the rest of the world was like anymore. Would we just simply have that one night to remember forever?

That was the big reason I didn't want to turn the radio on. I didn't know, and I was scared to know. What if everything back home was normal and our situation was a localized thing? I had to know eventually, but not just yet.

"Thank you," I told Denise.

"For what?" she asked.

"For everything," I told her, meaning it.

"You're goofy," she told me smiling lazily, her arms hugging her torso as the morning chill cut through our clothing.

"Usually."

"Look who's waiting for us," she said looking forward.

At the sandy landing, maybe half a mile ahead

of us across the open water, were two figures standing there, waving lazily.

"I wonder…"

"Let's just find out," I told her. "Let's not buy too much trouble."

"Or hope too much."

Brian and Tracy were smiling, waving at us lazily until we'd waved back in half a dozen different times. They were grinning ear to ear.

"Whoever was on the flare gun, that was awesome," I told them as soon as I cut the motor and let our momentum beach the boat.

"Tracy ran back to use the facilities and heard the jet."

"Did they, I mean are we…" Denise started.

"No, no. We just got up early to give Jordan and your sister some time alone."

Denise raised an eyebrow. If I wasn't mistaken, the look she was giving them was called the stink eye. It was a look I'd often gotten after telling Tracy how horrible her cooking was.

"She's a big girl. She's almost 27," Tracy said.

I'd never asked Denise her age, but as she was the older sister… I'd thought she was younger than that. Note to self, figure things out.

"Oh, I wasn't complaining," Denise said, "I'm sure they've snuck off into the bushes or meadow a couple times."

"As have we," Brian admitted. "There's just no

BOYD CRAVEN

privacy in a one room cabin."

The conversation was going places I didn't want to be involved in so I did what I always did; changed the subject.

"The radio wasn't a two-way, but it's an old shortwave. If the battery works, maybe we can listen in and see what's going on… if that plane put out the bat signal and a search party is coming."

Eyes shifted back to me and I grinned. Winning.

"You didn't try it out already?" Tracy asked me, "Why?"

"He had his hands full," Denise answered and Tracy nodded with a knowing grin.

Just like that, we were back at sex. What was I, 20 again?!

"I was worried that I wouldn't hear anything if it worked," I told them, "What if there isn't anybody out there?"

"But that jet had to have come from somewhere," Tracy pointed out.

"I know, I just wonder if it came from somewhere within range of our radio. We're pretty far north."

"There's the Ojibway reservation north of here," Denise told me, "I just thought of it, but they would have radio and off-grid facilities, wouldn't they?"

"I don't know much about them, but I thought about it a while back. Forgot about them actually."

"They bring in their supplies by DC-9s when the ice freezes up on the lakes. Our fly in guide said he did supply runs up there," Denise told us.

NORTHERN LIGHTS

"Is there any way to get there?" Brian asked me.

"To the tribal lands? I don't know where they are exactly. I don't have any maps and the GPS is fried."

"Yeah, but maybe after seeing the flares word has gotten back to them and maybe they'll be mounting a rescue mission," Tracy said staring into the sky.

I got out of the boat and held out my hand for Denise. She took it and stepped out herself. I grabbed the still zipped together and tied into a small package sleeping bags and our two backpacks. Denise grabbed a bucket that held the battery, the battery acid jug, and radio. She tried lifting two of the bundles of traps with her other hand but it was too much weight. She put one down.

"Hold on She-Ra, we're here to help," Tracy said and took what she could.

Together the girls started off down the trail. I stood there watching and thinking until they were out of sight.

"I'm assuming you had a good night, I mean, she seems happy. Why the hell are you looking so down?"

"What happens when we get rescued? That plane had to have seen us."

"What do you mean?" he asked me.

"Do Denise and Tonya go back to their old lives? What do we do?"

"We've changed a lot man; nothing is going to be the same," Brian said, the smile leaving his face, "And it's not just physical."

He was right, we'd all dropped a ton of weight, me probably more so than the rest of them because I was the heaviest of the group. I'd thought I had a good twenty or thirty of excess when we flew in, but I was pretty sure I was down way past that. It wasn't just starvation; it was a lack of variety and grueling labor every day.

"I know," I told him, "I mean, I can actually be in the same room with Tracy now and not want to pinch her head off."

"Yeah, I think you two argue now more out of habit than any real beef. That's not what I'm talking about overall, though. What's bugging you?"

I hesitated before answering, "Do you want to be rescued?"

A shocked look came over his features and he opened his mouth and closed it a couple times. Instead, I asked another question.

"If you could live today over and over and over, would you? Do you want to go back to the normal 9-5 job, the car payments, the headaches and everything else?"

"We have no idea what the winter's going to be like though," Brian told me, "We have no clue if we've put up enough food or not enough. These past few months have been relatively easy, but this is the tourist season up here. It gets bad."

"I know, I know," I told him, "It's just that everybody always asks me what I'm thinking, well, that's what I was thinking. If I could have yesterday and this morning to do over and over like that old movie Groundhog Day, I'd do it. When the snow falls,

NORTHERN LIGHTS

I'm probably going to be the first one to get cabin fever and dream about lovely Southern Michigan where it's warm and temperate winters don't dump eight feet of snow…"

"You're exaggerating now," he told me, "But I know what you mean. You worry too much."

"I know I do, but me being a worrywart is what led me to prepping."

"And your prepping and peepshow led you to meeting Denise, another fellow prepper. What are the chances of that, man?"

I thought about that. The chances of meeting someone, anyone, this far north and this remote was very small. I couldn't even find the cabin on my own last night so I could have been stuck up here for years if I hadn't walked upon Denise bathing on the Sandy Beach. And then to meet a woman my age roughly, who was also a prepper?

"Divine intervention," I made a half statement and question.

"Divine something," he said with a smile, and reached down to grab his portion of the load and walked back towards our camp.

After a moment, I followed.

After a week, our spirits had started to fall. After two weeks, we fell back into the normal routines we'd had. The two plastic garbage bins we'd buried were close to overflowing with food. We'd quit eating so much fresh food, even though it was available, and ate the oldest of the smoked fish. We learned quickly what spoilage looked like and made a pact to collect the big broad maple leaves whenever we could find them for the outhouse. Just in case. Nobody wanted to use snow in the middle of winter.

I also started a trap line, which was much more than the snares that would bring us in the occasional rabbit. In fact, the elk we got gave us so much meat, I pulled the trap line until we had smoked and dried everything we had. The one thing that really worried me, though, was the Dehydrator. It was not warm enough outside and didn't get warm enough inside the unit to effectively do its job, so we were left with the smoker.

I didn't want to ruin the dehydrator by converting it into a smoker, but after seeing part of the elk almost go to waste, we did it. I did save the screens and set those aside to be repurposed in the spring time if we were still here and Tracy, who'd become our resident weaver of cattail shoots, made us up more racks like was in the original smoker.

"You're just mad because we're going to have to clean the smoke residue from the inside," Tracy said on more than one occasion.

She was picking on me, but I just smiled. I was refusing to be baited because the winter was coming and I wanted to do everything I could to not have to get stuck in a cabin with three moody women. If we could change our habits of sniping at each other before that happened, maybe it would go peacefully.

NORTHERN LIGHTS

"Are you going to make some privacy panels?" Jordan asked her.

"Yeah, I've got one of them almost done now."

The panels were going to be in front of the three bunks. With it getting colder every day, privacy was becoming more and more scarce. Both Jordan and Tonya and then Brian and Tracy had made overnight trips to the other lake, but once the ice froze and the snow covered everything, we'd be locked in.

"You show me traps?" Tonya asked me suddenly.

"Sure. You mean the leg hold traps?" I asked her.

She made the yes motion that I'd come to associate with 'knock knock', only facing the tabletop.

"Sure thing, but maybe you ought to hold the gun on this trip," I said.

"I'm in," was chorused by everyone.

I couldn't blame them. I was pretty much recovered from my ordeal with the bear, and could go out more and do a lot more physically. Really, waiting for my hand to heal had been the worst, and the marks on my face took a while to heal.

"Somebody bring the flare gun then," I said, "Look what almost happened last time."

"Last time we got our hopes up," Tracy pointed out.

"Yeah, I don't know. I haven't seen any more planes," Brian piped in.

"How do you know they don't have a satellite beaming down at us?" Jordan asked.

"Oh God, I hope not... we've been using the

sandy beach to wash up," Denise said poking me in the side.

"Well, it's not only for bathing…" I slipped up and said, and everybody grinned.

We were back to talking about sex again. Dammit. I couldn't believe I'd done that.

"Sure, I'm going to check on the traps in an hour or so, or we could all just go now?" I said.

They loved the idea so we all headed out. I set my trap line near where the bear had attacked me. For small game, the meadow would be a perfect place for them to hide and feed. There was plenty of busy blueberry plants to hide within and where there was small game, there was larger game. I was hoping to start trapping Mink, Lynx and other fur-bearers with some of the larger traps because none of us had coats… Just a couple sweaters apiece.

I made sure the camp gun was on safe and gave it to Tonya.

"Make sure if something is eating my face to do what you did last time," I told her and she grinned.

"Make sure to run the next time you see a bear, don't tackle it," Denise told me.

Oh, it was going to be fun!

We went past the snare lines and, in the last one, the one that we were getting bait for when the bear attacked, was a nice fat rabbit. Tonya squealed in excitement and rushed to reset the trap if the line wasn't messed up. Sometimes when using snares, the line gets damaged, but rabbits are generally not that hard on the lines. Snares are usually dispos-able, one-use items, especially for medium to larger animals that put a kink in the line.

I explained this to everyone, but it was the second or third time I'd told it to Tonya. She'd been fascinated with the trapping aspect, which surprised me. She didn't like to hunt so much, but she was learning how to spot game trails and I'd given her several snares for her to try different trapping techniques of her own. With the cable and supplies we had from the crashed plane, I wasn't going to run out soon.

"Ok, so I marked the trail out with orange streamers for the trap line," I told them as we got to the meadow.

"Like you did the trail going to the beach?" Tracy asked.

"Yeah. I put them high up in the trees so it won't startle or scare small game."

"What are you trapping for?" Brian asked me.

"Right now? Honestly, fur-bearing animals and anything that we can use." I answered.

I'd brought along a couple extra traps just in case one of the anchoring lines came loose or a trap was lost.

After five minutes of hiking up the meadow, I pointed out the first streamer off to the left. It had been a hard place to start the trap line because it was where I was standing when I noticed the bear charging up the hill towards Tonya. Still, what I'd noticed was all the small game trails. Until we had enough furs dried, scraped and smoked, we weren't going to make a batch of tanning solution and a few more rabbits would make it enough to try it out.

"There's an orange streamer," Brian said pointing further down the small trail.

"That's the first trap set," I told them.

We walked up and I stopped in front of it.

"Where's the trap?" Tracy asked, crowding in behind me.

"See that shiny circle of metal?" I asked her.

"Yeah?"

"It's right under that. I covered it up loosely with dirt and leaves."

"What is that, a piece of metal?" she asked.

"Yeah, I cut it out of an old can and rubbed the corrosion off on a rock to make it shiny. Raccoons like shiny stuff so the idea is he walks up, reaches to grab it…" and I poked the shiny metal disk with a stick and the trap sprang, snapping the dry stick in two.

"That's just going to cut their hands off," Tracy said, disgust in her voice.

"No, a dried stick isn't as tough as bone. It doesn't break anything, just holds them until I come along."

"And do what?" Jordan asked me.

"Pop them in the head with the .22 or club them," I admitted.

"Club them?" Denise asked me.

"Well, I haven't yet but, if you aim right, one blow breaks the neck and they're just as dead as getting shot with a .22," I said, hoping she wasn't disgusted with me.

"If I run my own traps, I'm borrowing the gun, I'm not sure if I can bop a rabbit in the head," Denise said.

"It isn't for everybody," I admitted. "But we've only got so much ammunition. There may come a day where…"

"We know Brian," Tracy said, coming to my defense.

Her husband nodded at her as if to say he agreed. Then I showed them how to reset it. With the trap sprung, I moved it and then used my hand to push aside the loose soil and leaves, leaving a shallow depression on the forest floor. Then I showed them how the two bars on either side of the jaws worked. You press down on one, and the other hooks to the trigger which holds the jaws down. Since the one we were looking at was already anchored with a cable to the tree, I just pointed out how I did that.

The hard part was the sifting and covering the trap. New traps are almost useless. They smell like cutting oil and there isn't a lick of corrosion on them. Any metal the animals encounter is going to be rusted to some degree or another, and the rust actually helps camouflage the traps some, as long as it isn't deeply pitted. Still, it wasn't enough sometimes. That's why I started pushing sand in the edges of the shallow depression until the trap was filled up to the edge of the jaws and the trigger.

Then I just took handfuls and slowly let it tumble from my fingers. I'd been snapped before, and it hurts. I didn't want my friends to see that happen to me, so I took my time. When that was done, I used a stick flat against the ground to sort of smooth things over a little bit without putting pressure near the trigger. Lastly was leaves and the shiny round piece of metal.

"That's pretty slick. Does it work for more than small animals?" Brian asked when I was done.

"That works for pretty much all animals," I told him. "I didn't do a lot of fur trapping as a kid, but I've read about it—"

"In a book, or watched a YouTube video," they all chorused and I grinned.

"Yeah," I admitted, turning red.

Apparently I'd used that line a bit, but it was true. Sometimes there was no way a person could have hands-on knowledge of everything. That's the beauty of books and reading about things. I knew they were more picking on me more than disparaging my methods, so I just gave them a grin and showed them where the next traps were.

We spent the rest of the afternoon doing that and, after the third set, Denise suggested I let everyone take a turn setting off and resetting the traps. She had better insight than I did and I totally should have done that from the outset. The last trap was triggered and dirt was everywhere, but there was no animal.

"What happened here?" Jordan asked, but it was his woman who answered.

Tonya had blossomed from a shy woman into a very outgoing one. She could follow spoken conversation by lip reading and she quit being shy and started using her own voice to communicate with us when it was the whole group. Instead, she saw something and walked over to the tree the anchor cable was strapped to.

She laid her hand out, showing everyone the deep scratch marks on the bark and turned to me and placed her hand on the scarred side of my face. I shivered. A bear had set off the trap. It probably triggered it with one massive paw and tried to push the tree over before it just pulled the trap off. I knelt down and found some black hairs on the forest floor about three feet away and held a small tuft of it up, showing everyone.

"It's that last bear," Brian said.

"Let's go," Tonya said suddenly, startling everyone.

I decided right then and there that I wasn't going to be scared off.

"No, let's set up another trap," I said.

Everyone looked at me funny but they all took several steps back, probably scared I was going to do something stupid. I took off my daypack and pulled out one of the large cable snares I'd made up in the cabin. The loop on it was pretty large, the cable pretty stiff. I figured out my height and attached it to the heavier cable at the base of the tree where the rabbit was, and then pulled a roll of cotton string out of my pocket.

It was something I always carried. It was more like yarn than mason's line, but I'd always used the green filament for this sort of thing. I lightly tied the open end of the loop with a box knot and then stretched the line over to another tree. Next, I made the loop the size I wanted again, and tied a piece of string with the same kind of knot near the cam locks on the snare and tied the other end higher up on the tree. Now the loop was anchored to the tree near the base of it, and the loop was open into the game trail at the height I thought the bear was going to be when walking on all fours. Now, for bait…

"The string won't cause the snare to hang up?" Jordan asked.

"With something as heavy as the bear, it's used to pushing through brush. It'll break that string easily. With rabbit snares, I use something lighter, sometimes long stalks of dried grass." I told them, "But we've got to bait this one."

"With what?" Denise asked.

"Part of your sister's rabbit," I told them.

They looked at me surprised, but I shrugged. It was something I'd done countless times. I tied a heavier line of paracord around a tree branch, at a little over eye level height, with a bow knot, then I tied it to one leg of the rabbit, behind the foot joint. Next I made a slit around both feet and sliced straight down the leg towards the stomach area. I joined them with a Y and made a shallow cut down to the neck.

Tonya was watching me especially closely. She hadn't done it before and I offered her the knife and she nodded. She'd seen me do it, but I'm not a great teacher. I should have been teaching them some of the stuff instead of just showing them. She made a scissor motion to the rabbit's front paws and I nodded, finding the joint and showing her. She nodded and worked, separating the foot from the leg. Then she did the other side and made similar cuts to the back legs, connecting them to the slit just below the neck. Then she cut out the tail and the rear end and started pulling.

She'd seen me do this and it surprised me to see she already had a handle on it since it wasn't something I'd ever seen her do. The skin separated as she pulled, and the hide separated from around the legs with some heavy pulling. Not all of the guts fell out when she did that, but it opened the cavity. She stopped pulling when the hide was down by the head.

"Now cut it there," I told her pointing to the neck.

She hadn't been squeamish about the warm wet inside of the hide thus far, but her face looked mildly disgusted as she used my belt knife to sever the head. It came off with the pelt. I took the hide and draped it over a tree limb and pointed for her to go on. She handed me back the knife and reached in and pulled out the entrails. I stopped her, showing her the heart and liver, which we kept in a plastic bag.

I thought I was going to be grossing everyone out, but I heard somebody's stomach gurgle behind me. I turned to see if I was going to get puked on, but when I looked, everyone was just watching, waiting. She finished gutting the rabbit and handed me the knife. I separated the head from the hide and kicked all the guts and head into a pile in front of the snare.

"And bears eat that?" Jordan asked me, not a trace of disgust on his face.

"I don't know, honestly. I think they eat anything and everything. This time of year, they have to be almost ready to hibernate, right?" I asked.

"I don't know. I kind of thought that they had moved on. After the kid killed momma bear, we only saw the one other bear."

"Maybe something happened to them?" I asked.

"Maybe a dominant male came in and ran out all the others," Denise said.

That made my blood run cold. I didn't know how big a range bears had, but being close to a lake was probably well within their daily travels for water and easy food. Also the berries. I hadn't noticed any more bears when I set the traps up, but who said I had to be on their schedule to see them? Maybe they started out earlier or later than me. Maybe a giant male bear had been watching me from the gloom of some felled tree, waiting for me to not notice so it could creep up and….

I jumped as Denise poked me. I put my knife in my sheath and bent down to wipe off the blood on my fingers with the leaves and dirt of the soil.

"You were thinking something creepy, weren't you?" she asked.

"Yeah, that I was going to be a chicken nugget if a big bear happened to walk by."

"Don't worry, I'll protect you," Tonya said, drying her hands in the dirt the same way I just had.

"Question," Tracy asked, "won't you be leaving your scent behind when you do that?"

"Yeah, yeah I will. I don't think the animals up here have much human interaction. They probably figure we're just some hairless bipeds who live near a tiny spot at the lake. We're really not hunting them and the traps might smell like us for a time, though. I don't think those rabbit guts have a chance to go to waste, though. Those three bears were opportunists."

Boy was I right.

CHAPTER 16

We found when we returned to the cabin that both smokers had been ransacked. We couldn't tell which food had been half eaten, and what had fallen into the dirt. The plastic melted up into a charred mess, and we had to reset the stakes and make new supports. Our smokers weren't bear proof and while we had been out trapping, the bear had waltzed in and helped itself to a ton of food, ruining our setup in the process.

We rebuilt them, using the last of the plastic and a piece of canvas we found in the old trapper's cabin. I think it was part of a shelter half, but I'd never taken the time to figure it out. A few days later, we were going full steam again, but we agreed that somebody was going to stay at the cabin at all times in the future, and at least shout or rattle pots and pans from inside the window to try to scare them off.

When our wood pile was almost 7' tall, 15' wide across the back of the cabin and almost seven feet deep, we quit splitting wood. Instead, we started dragging chunks close to the cabin, where we could find them easily in the snow. The days were becoming very short, and the nights were long. The first morning that we woke up to a skim of ice on the water had me suddenly worried I'd waited too long to do the tanning. I gathered up all the furs and rinsed them out on the dock. Normally they'd be salted, but we didn't have salt when we first started out. We'd found a couple bags of salt at the trapping cabin, though, coarse salt, but a lot of it.

I used a printed out set of instructions in my binder from Mother Earth News to start the process. I didn't have baking soda, but I had baking powder. Without Google, I didn't know if that'd be a good idea or not, but I did it anyways. I mixed the salt into a boiling pot of water until it was dissolved. The recipe called for pickling or Kosher salt, that's fine salt, and I needed the solution more than the fine texture so I dissolved it. I used one of the old steel drums we'd brought back from the last trip and I put everything in to soak.

Denise had joined me and was smiling.

"Looking forward to your bearskin coat?" she asked.

"No, I'd like a bearskin rug, in front of a roaring fire, a glass of wine and—"

"Don't go all crazy, little ears," Tonya interrupted, "it's my sister."

I stuck my tongue out at her and she returned the gesture.

"How do you know when it's done?" Denise asked me.

"We'll have to experiment, I've never done this before. I'm winging it a lot here," I told her.

"It looks like it'll be good for an overcoat material," she said smiling.

"I hope so."

"So now what?" Jordan asked.

"What do you mean?" I asked him.

"We're almost ready for the winter time. Should we start filling the inside with logs for the fire? Leave them outside…? We've got enough fish and meat jerky to last us a bit… What else can we do?"

"I don't know," I told him honestly, "run the trap lines, I guess, and try to stay healthy. One day we're going to try to open the door and it's probably going to have snow piled up. We'll have a lot of downtime."

"This has almost been like a dream," Denise said, running her hand down my arm.

"It has been. I just wish that radio would have worked." I told her.

I had no way of knowing if the battery was just too far gone, or whether the radio had been fried by the EMP. Still, I was having second thoughts about not knowing.

"Me too," they both said.

"You know, we ought to do something fun for once," I told them.

"For once?" Denise asked me, an eyebrow arched, "I don't know, I think we've had some fun," she said with a grin.

"No, I mean… We kinda missed out on a lot this year. Halloween was last month and it's got to be closer to thanksgiving than not. We should do a holiday party of some kind."

"You, my friend, are loco," Brian said coming up, "but I like it."

"Hey, I found a tree where turkeys have been roosting," Tracy told me.

"What?" My head whipped around so hard it cracked.

"Mashed potatoes and gravy, a deep fried turkey, sweet potato pie, rolls and stuffing and…" Denise was going on and on so I stopped her words by pulling her close and clamping my hand over her mouth.

"Where is it?" I asked her.

"Not far from the first snare set."

"Why didn't we hear them?" I wondered aloud.

"You know what they sound like?" Brian asked me.

"I've never hunted turkeys," I admitted. "But I know what a tom is supposed to sound like."

"A tom is supposed to sound like a tom," Denise said in a mock voice like mine.

I was still holding her close so I tickled her ribs, which had become more pronounced, and she twisted and writhed.

"I know where you sleep," she hissed more than once.

"That sounds good then," I told them. "We'll go figure out how to find a turkey and get it baked. That is as long as Tracy agrees—"

"Not to cook it?" she asked, her expression immediately going pouty one hand cocked on her hip.

"No, help out with cooking it. Your mother had the best turkey ever. Remember? The year we had it at her house?"

"Is that a compliment?" she asked, her eyebrows almost touching her hairline.

"No." Brian whispered into her ear, "That's him setting you up to get even for throwing him off the boat this summer."

"Oh yeah, hey, I forgot about that," I said, grinning broadly.

"You can sleep in the outhouse tonight," she said, pointing at Brian who was cracking up.

"Ok, so let's go find these turkeys."

That wasn't meant to be funny, but Brian laughed even louder and soon everyone else but me was rolling.

I wouldn't let everyone come as a large group to recon the tree. It would have been too much noise and too much motion and scent. What I knew about turkey hunting, of course, came from reading, but also from talking to my father. He'd always told me that whenever he was hunting deer and didn't have a tag, turkeys would walk up. When he was turkey hunting, he'd have deer come up and sniff him. As soon as you have that magical license to kill, they knew it somehow.

I did not, in fact, have a license to kill, so I hoped I'd have one eating out of my hand as I clubbed it and threw it in a baking pot. That didn't happen.

"Over there," she said.

I followed her hand and saw the tree. Its branches were at least twenty feet off the ground.

"I was looking for a spot close to the cabin for Brian and me to have some alone time. It was almost dark and I saw them flying up into the tree. Their wings made such a loud noise I'm surprised that it didn't scare everything out of the woods. It's startled me, that's for sure."

"So that's where they go to sleep?" I asked her.

"Yeah, I checked it out again last night. I don't know when they fly down, but it looks like they're digging through the leaves here for something."

She was right; the leaf litter was dug up. We walked over and I saw some short, bushier looking trees. It was hard to tell what it was without the leaves, but it wasn't something I recognized. I kicked some leaf litter out of the way and found four tan colored nuts.

"Is that a walnut?" Tracy asked me as I knelt and picked them up.

"No, walnuts have that green shell around them. Also, they put off something in the soil that prevents other things from growing around them. These bushy trees are all around here."

Here was a small opening in the trees. It was caused by the taller tree that the turkeys had been roosting in, but smaller brush had been growing nearby and under it.

"Beechnut!" Tracy said snapping her fingers.

"No, I don't think they are that."

I used my knife to clean off the outside edge. Was this the nut, or the outer shell? Was it poisonous?

I used the base of one of the shorter trees to be on one side and I pressed my blade into the shell of the nut, cutting it in half. I smelled it and although it had a familiar scent, I couldn't place it.

"What do you think?" I asked, holding a half out to Tracy.

"I think you're too scared to try it. It's not poison."

"How would you know?" I asked her.

"The turkeys are eating them, dummy. Maybe that's why they are so close?" she said.

She had a point.

"We'll both take a bite."

"Together," she said, "On three."

"Fine. One, two, three," I said and bit into the kernel within the half shell, expecting the worst.

"Hazelnut!" Tracy said, pumping her fist up in the air, and pushed the whole thing into her mouth.

"Wow," I said following suit.

She was right. Now I had to figure out if I wanted to gather nuts that had fallen sometime in the fall, or hunt turkeys.

"Want to get everybody else?" she asked.

"You just want us to figure out how to make a Nutella for you."

NORTHERN LIGHTS

"You better believe it," she said, and started walking out of the trail.

I turned and looked at the tree and the spots beneath it that had been scratched bare. Winter was coming and we desperately needed something, anything, to bridge the gap. The nuts would provide an essential fat and oil that we'd probably been missing, so after the hunt, we'd all come and gather them if there were any left.

CHAPTER 17

We'd found out that week by trial and error that roasting the nuts gave them a better flavor and made them easier to crack. The bottom two shelves of the smokers we usually reserved for slow cooking meat, but they were full of the filberts, or hazelnuts when the smoker was in use. Tracy had been correct, the birds had moved into the area to collect their bounty. She'd also suggested we watch the rest of the wildlife and see what they were doing.

She'd found several hickory and walnut trees by watching the squirrels. I don't know why I hadn't thought about it, but to be honest, I was ready for some variety in our diet. When I mentioned that aloud Denise had gone to my binder and pulled out a section on wild foraging. The first frost hadn't killed everything off, but it had started to come close. She was going to go foraging for greens and onions with her sister. I wanted to go, but there was something they wanted to talk about and I, of course, assumed it was about Jordan and me.

They left with conspiratorial looks towards the trail leading back to the old cabins and I stood there a moment before sitting down at the picnic table.

"You look like somebody just shot your dog," Brian said sitting down.

"Naw, it's not that, just thinking."

"About what?" Tracy said, joining him in the seat across from me.

Jordan picked that moment to show up and he walked over and sat down too.

"They going back to the old cabin?" he asked.

"They didn't say, said they had something to talk about," I told everyone.

"They're going to go visit their parents," Tracy said.

I hadn't expected that, but it made sense.

"They were talking about it last night. With the cold coming, the ice might freeze up and if it's their last chance to do it before winter…"

"They taking the power boat?" I asked.

"Probably. Denise knows how to use it," Brian told me.

"Not much gas left," I said.

There had been two five gallon cans of gas when we'd started the trip. We'd used most of that over summer and fall. We had maybe a gallon and a half after what was left in the tank.

"We have enough. The way it's been getting, I expect it to snow soon," Brian told me.

"And snow and ice will lock us all in," Jordan said.

"We could make snow shoes," I said grinning.

"Considering our shoes are falling apart, I'm not against that. How's the leather coming?"

The bear hide hadn't been salted or smoked right away, so instead of having a nice coat out of it, it had turned into a nice big piece of leather, after all, the fur fell out. The rest of the tanning had gone well and we were stretching and softening the hides.

"I'd say it's just about done. We should be able to make stuff from it at any time." I told them.

"What are you thinking about to sew this stuff up for?" Tracy asked.

"Using a leather punch and then thin strips of leather?" I said not sure.

"Why not use the suture needle to make a hole and pull fishing line through it? Wouldn't that be tighter?" Jordan asked.

"Dude, that's brilliant, I could kiss you," I said pulling him to me in a mock hug and making a kissy face.

"Easy there, man, our girls have only been gone for a minute," he said, pushing me back, "no need to resort to that."

"No really, that's a great idea," Tracy said.

"I don't know how to sew," I told them. "But it sounds like the doc here just found his new calling."

"Hey, don't you be volunteering me for everything," Jordan complained, but he was smiling.

"We need to get our clothes washed out before the lake freezes up too," I told everyone. "I think we can measure it in days now and not weeks."

"Yeah, I thought you were getting a bit ripe," Tracy said.

"That's just your breath," I snapped back.

"Ok, come on," Brian said holding a hand up, "We went almost a month without this…"

I smiled and we talked. There wasn't much on the smoker. The fish had moved into the deeper water of the lake and getting to them had turned into a chore, especially with the wind kicking up and pushing the boat around. Without using the motor, it would be hard and it was bone chilling. We'd relied on the trapping for our daily meat and the ladies had started getting greens, wild leeks and little things they could find to go with the dwindling staples of rice and beans. We probably had a month left of those until we had to start living off wild foods completely…

We'd washed our clothing off the dock. There was a large rock near it that you could lean over and reach the shore. We'd get our clothing wet, push it up on the rock and use soap and work it in through the clothing. We figured that working it in by hand was probably better than the agitation anyways and we'd rinse it out with lake water and hang it up to dry on a tree branch somewhere. There never was a shortage of wind, but if we had to worry about the clothes freezing before drying…

"We're almost there," Brian told me.

"Almost where?" I asked him.

"The point where we're as prepared as we're going to be and the snow is going to shut us all down."

"We can still do the trapping," I told him.

"True, but they haven't been producing much," Tracy said.

"That damned bear is scaring everything off," I said.

That was a sore spot for me. The bear never went back to where that large snare was. I'd found evidence of him walking down that game trail where the trap line was set. Once in a while, I'd find a track or a scratch on the tree but no visible sign. I didn't know when they were supposed to go into hibernation, but if he was the one scaring off game, then he should go to sleep already.

"Maybe we should set more traps for it?" Tracy asked.

"We don't even know if there is another bear. Have you seen it?" Brian asked me.

"I saw tracks, scratches high up on the trees. Once a pile of scat."

"Scat?" Tracy asked.

"Bear shit," I told her.

"So it's true then?" she said, half statement, half question.

"What's true?" I asked.

"That a bear DOES shit in the woods."

I put my head down as everyone laughed. With what we'd found in the way of wild nuts, the dried meat, fish, blueberries and everything else, I thought probably we had enough to make it until

NORTHERN LIGHTS

March. Maybe. Four months until starvation. What would happen the next winter? If we got lucky with trapping over the winter it would stretch, and we had food that we'd all brought, food the girls' family had brought, and food from the trapper cabin. It still wasn't enough for the six of us. Next year we wouldn't have that extra.

I started to mentally go over what we would need to do and made a note to myself to see if there were forage items in the spring we could get close by as we waited for the ice to melt enough to take a boat in.

"So, has Denise been throwing up in the morning lately?" Tracy asked.

The question threw me. She had, just a couple of times.

"Yeah, why?" I asked her.

Tracy gave me a big grin and then turned to look at Jordan, "Have you noticed it too?" she asked.

"Denise has, but nobody else. Why…? Oh shit," Jordan said a look of amused horror on his face.

He looked like the kids do when they go on a scary roller coaster. Both terrified and having the time of their lives.

"What?" I asked.

"Nothing," Tracy said, "probably something she ate."

"We all eat the same stuff," I told her.

It was true, a very boring and repetitive diet if you want to be honest here.

"Probably didn't agree with her. That's all."
"What…"

It hit me.

"You think?" I asked her.

"A girl knows these things," she said smiling.

"But you've never—"

"I can't have kids," Brian said. "We've tried."

"Oh, I'm sorry man, I didn't mean—"

"No, it's ok." Tracy said, "Still, a girl knows these things. I think she's wondering herself."

"So are they really going to visit their parents'?" I asked her.

"Yeah, and probably get some sister time in. If we ever get out of here, I'm going to see if I can ever find my half-sister."

"You have a half-sister?" I asked her.

I thought I knew a lot about her, but this was news to me.

"Yeah, I guess my dad was married before, back when we lived in Washington State. Had a daughter he didn't know about. They got divorced and then his ex-wife found out she was pregnant."

"Wow, I bet that was a surprise for you," I told her.

"Yeah, I found her through Facebook and we started talking. I was going to see about visiting her in the spring time…"

Her words trailed off. She was thinking what we all were. Nothing was the same and spring was a while away still.

"Let's just hope somebody flies over again," Brian said.

"That didn't work out so well last time," I told him.

NORTHERN LIGHTS

"Maybe they couldn't stop, or they didn't have anybody else in the area who could stop?"

"Maybe. How long do we give the girls before we go check on them?" I asked Jordan.

"Five hours or so," he said. "Then I'll go wait on the beach and see."

I thought it over and nodded.

CHAPTER 18

Did I even mention how much I hate the cold? We'd somewhat lost track of what day it was, but it was getting close to Christmas, or thereabouts. My problem was we didn't spend enough time and effort topping off the cistern. The filtration system separated the lake gunk out from the water so everything that was in the cabin would be clean. That was why I was outside with the axe, dulling it against what I'd found to be at least eight inches of ice – and counting.

I would work for a time until I was just about sweating, swinging and chopping a spot to the side of the dock and then I'd go inside and trade out with somebody else. They would do the same. After the three of us guys all took a turn, Tracy broke through and brought the first bucket of slushy water and poured it into the filtrations intake. When that was done she went out for one more bucket, wearing the fur-lined leather jacket that was made from a hodgepodge. We'd put the fur on the inside, and the bear leather on the outside. It turned out warm, but it was ugly as all get out.

I'd considered making a raccoon hat to go with it, but I'd not run into any of the critters. The good news, though, the trap line was starting to produce again. I'd even snared a lynx a week before.

"Your turn," Tracy said stopping and Denise stood.

Her tummy didn't have a noticeable bump, but I noticed it when we were in our sleeping bags stomach to stomach.

"I can probably do one or two," she said and donned the gear and headed out.

"How cold is it out there?" Jordan asked, standing in front of the wood stove.

"-10 Fahrenheit," Tracy said, her teeth chattering.

"Wow, that's…" I started to say.

Tonya pulled a sleeping bag around her shoulders and mock shivered.

"I checked the thermometer when I bought the last bucket in," she said.

The door to the cabin burst open and Denise dropped the empty bucket just inside the door.

"There's a plane! Hurry!"

We all looked at each other and then everyone was running out into the freezing temperatures. It was snowing again, the large flakes coming down silently, coating everything in a thick blanket. I had missed out on grabbing the flare gun on my way out because Tracy had snatched it first. We had two shells.

"Where is it?" I screamed, running out onto the dock and onto the ice.

"I can hear it!" Brian yelled and then pointed to the north-west.

Tracy ran out onto the ice near me. We'd all avoided the hole by the dock and the rest of the group followed after her. She took aim and send a red flare almost straight up into the sky. Through the swirling snowstorm, the flare shot up like a rocket into the sky. It lit up everything around us and I could see halfway across the lake. The other thing I noticed? A red blinking light of some sort of airplane marker lights.

"Shoot another one!" Brian shouted.

"I'm going to wait a second. Let this one fall before I do," she screamed, the wind almost taking her words away from her.

"The plane is banking," Jordan screamed.

Tonya was looking around at us, the snow starting to stick in her hair. She was laughing and crying. Tracy shot off another flare a minute later. It seemed even brighter and we could make out the shape of the nose; not just from the light, but because it was turning our direction.

"When that flare goes out they're not going to have any point of reference!" I screamed.

I started running and was soon joined by Denise.

NORTHERN LIGHTS

"What are you doing?" she screamed.

"We need fire or something else to get their attention," I screamed into the wind, "everything is white down here right now."

"I'll get some wood!" Denise yelled.

I ran inside. We had enough gasoline left to splash around in the bottom of the fuel can. I grabbed sleeping bags, and the can of fuel and tore off out the door. Denise was already ahead of me, half a dozen split logs in her arms. She stumbled and righted herself before I could catch up with her. It was a wild crazy run that had me almost crying with anticipation.

Denise dropped the wood near where we all had been standing on the ice and collapsed. I threw a sleeping bag at her and the rest to the others and dumped the gasoline over the pile of wood. I felt around in my pocket for a lighter, or a book of matches.

"What is it?" Brian asked, probably asking me what I needed.

"Fire, I need to light this up!"

It was almost comical. Everyone patted their pockets looking for a lighter when Denise sat up and took off her necklace and handed it to me. It was one of those push button sparkers. She'd showed us how to start a fire with it. I took it and knelt down in the snow and ice, soaking my pants through completely.

"It's got propellers," Jordan screamed.

It was getting close if he could make it out in this storm; I couldn't hear anything myself. I pressed the ignitor against the log and pushed. Sparks shot out all over, but no fire. I wasn't worrying about the big whoosh as the gas went up, as long as I had flames. I pressed again and again. When it lit, I pulled my arm back. Luckily I was wearing a sweater or I may have gotten my arm hairs singed off.

"Is the ice thick enough?" Jordan screamed to me.

"I don't know. It should be," I yelled back, my voice going hoarse.

I took the end of the sleeping bag that Denise offered me and pulled her close. Even though she was wet and cold, her warmth was amazing. We all huddled close to the fire, watching. The plane banked again, turning, and started flying to the southwest again.

"Oh God, do you think they saw us?" I asked them.

"They did. I don't know what they are doing, though."

The plane was low enough that we could almost make out the tail numbers, but the snow kept hitting me in the face and eyes.

"It's turning again," Tracy screamed.

I saw the landing gear come out. I couldn't tell if it was skids or tires and suddenly having a fire on the ice as who knows how much weight and force was going to be bearing down on us and the surface of the ice didn't seem like such a great idea. I started backing up, and soon we all were running back to the dock. I almost went into the hole we chopped earlier because I wasn't paying attention and had slowed to look backward but was pulled sideways by Tracy who just gave me a mischievous grin.

"Is this ice thick enough?" Tonya asked.

"I don't know," her sister yelled.

Standing on the dock, I felt the wood tremble as the plane touched down at the far end of the lake, a thousand yards away from us. Suddenly I wondered: how do you stop a plane that's just landed on ice? How far would it slide?

The pilot was sitting at the kitchen table as we packed, looking around the place in shock. We'd met him at the plane and he'd quickly advised us to head inside where we could hear and be heard better.

"So you're telling me you've been up here alone since July?" he asked.

"Yeah," Tracy said, "we'd just gotten here when the EMP happened."

"You know about the EMP?" the pilot asked.

He was British by the sound of it, but I didn't want to ask where he was from considering we were all packing our gear and heading south and west.

"Educated guess," I told him, "our pilot's pacemaker blew out, and all the electronic stuff we had got fried. The pilot saw a big flash before he died. Must have been bad."

"You don't know the half of it," the pilot said, "I'm bloody glad you put up the flare, there wouldn't have been another supply drop for six months or more."

"You were up at the reservation?" Tracy asked.

"Right you are," Patrick, the pilot said, "They're set pretty good up there… now, now, you don't have to double and triple layer up, I've got heat in most of the cockpit area," he said to Brian.

"We've only got one coat between us," Tracy said.

"Bloody hell. Three couples up here for almost eight months and no coat? It's the Arctic for Christ's sake!"

"We didn't come here in the winter time… Wait, you said eight months?!"

We all looked at each other in shock. It was almost January. Christmas was sometime this week, wasn't it?

"Today's February the thirteenth. Tomorrow is Valentine's day."

My eyes crossed trying to figure out how I could have lost that much time.

"Right then, got everything you want?"

"Do we need to bring any food?" I asked him.

"Not unless you need to eat in the next few hours. Winds are with us and as long as there aren't any issues with icing, our first stop is in Winnipeg."

"First stop?" I ask.

"Yeah, I'm picking up a load, refueling and heading for Anchorage," he said.

We were putting on every article of clothing we had and shoving last minute essentials into our sleeping bags. We were leaving behind a lot, though. It hurt to do it, but we were safe.

NORTHERN LIGHTS

"How bad is it in America?" I asked him.

His eyes found mine, and I could see the truth in them.

"I'm from the Flint area in Michigan," I told him.

"Flint's gone," he said. "One of the first cities to burn down. The survivors were bussed out of town if you believe the papers."

"Oh man," I said, not knowing what to think of everything.

"I can take you with me and drop you off at one of my next two stops, up to you, but I'm not heading towards Michigan. The USA is in a world of hurt currently. Alaska and the Pacific Northwest like Washington are the only areas not in total anarchy and chaos. Their power grids didn't get knocked out."

"Washington?" Tracy asked and then looked at her husband.

"We'll get on the trip to Alaska," Brian told Patrick.

"Where do you want to go?" I asked Denise.

Jordan too was staring at the girls, one to the other. We were probably thinking the same thing. Was this it?

"Wherever you are," Denise told me, burying her face in my neck in a fierce hug.

"Right then, let's get a move on, shall we? My co-pilot's likely to come out here looking for me and cock something up."

I laughed. It was just too surreal.

BOYD CRAVEN

We'd been in the air for an hour. One of the quirks our pilot had was collecting newspapers. He said in a day's time he could fly from mainland to Alaska in one long string. Even if everybody was reporting on the same story, every geographical location had their own slant, their own view or new information one of them didn't. He hadn't been flying at all the past week, so the papers we were reading were from two weeks ago, dated February 1st.

"America At War," one read. "80% mortality as exceptionally strong winter storms move through North America," read another.

"80% mortality?" I asked Patrick, walking towards the cockpit for some more warmth.

Here's a little hint, cargo planes aren't built like passenger liners where there are seat heaters, personal lights, and air conditioners. You sit as close to the cockpit as you can and shiver in the sleeping bags and clothing. It was too cramped for six of us to be in there at once, so we hung back near the doorway.

"I heard it was worse," David, Patrick's co-pilot said.

"Worse?" I asked, not quite believing it.

"You should hear this bloke from Kentucky. He's on the shortwave… sorry, forgot, no radio for you… Uh…" he broke off as he got a good look at my face. "Bloody hell, what happened to you?"

Tracy stood up and moved behind me and answered before I could say anything. "He saved one of us by tackling a bear and killing it with his knife."

Both pilots cursed, and I turned around to tell Tracy what a liar she was when we hit a little turbulence. I got a good look and everyone behind me in the cramped hallway to the cargo hold was smiling or cracking up.

"Took on a bear with a knife. No wonder these folks did ok up here on their own."

"That guy's from Flint, Michigan," Patrick said, pointing at me.

I opened my mouth to say something, but David made the sign of the cross and I paused then took a breath.

"I heard about Flint, it's ok. I'm not going back."

"No, I wasn't uh… I heard Flint was pretty rough, even before the whole end of the world thing," David told me.

"Honestly," I said, "now? I think I'm better off wrestling another bear than going back there."

"Right you are, right you are. Any of you have family you want us to radio ahead for?"

"We're all kind of orphans," Tracy said. "Unless you can get a message to somebody in Washington state?"

"I can try, Miss. Once we land in Winnipeg you can call them maybe?"

"That would be great. Let me write down what I know…" Tracy grabbed the flight log and got a blank page near the back and wrote down the details and handed it back to him.

"Not much to go on, but we can try," Patrick told her after reading the note.

"Trying is all we've been doing since July," Tracy told him and headed back.

After a moment, I followed as well.

"Tomorrow is Valentine's day," I said, crawling into the 2 sleeping bags Denise and I had zipped together.

"So, what's your point?" she asked.

"What do you want for Valentine's day?" I asked her, kissing her on the nose.

"Change of plans," David said, one ear covered from the headphones. "We're the last flight into Winnipeg. Bad storm front coming in. We're going to have to stay the night and fly out in the morning. When we told the flight controllers about finding you, they said they have four rooms at the local hotel for us. Will that work?"

"I'd love it," I called back and kissed Denise again.

"Spending Valentine's day in a hotel room? Our own bed, by ourselves…"

"Oy, let's not make it pornographic in here will ya, I got flying to do," Patrick yelled.

Why did it always come back to that?

"We don't mind. It'll be nice to get someplace that has central heat!"

"Do they have fast food there in Winnipeg?" Jordan yelled.

Suddenly I was ravenous, achingly hungry for a double cheeseburger.

"Yeah, you blokes hungry? There's a McDonalds in the airport lounge. I could stop in and get you all a few McDoubles , seeing as you haven't had

NORTHERN LIGHTS

a proper meal in a while."

"I think I love him as much as I love you right now," I told Denise.

"Oy, oy, don't do that, we're flying here," David yelled, frustrated.

I wasn't being bad, but I'd been tackled by my girlfriend inside the confines of the sleeping bag. I'd ended up pinned to the wall with her holding me face to face. I smiled.

"I can be very persuasive,"

"Little eyes," Tonya yelled, and we all laughed.

We'd figure out what would come next. Somehow, some way. We'd survived so long on our own. Thin, but not starved, rich in spirit, and with a will to live. We would find a way, and as long as we had each other, we would never be defeated. Ahead of us, outside of the cockpit, the Northern Lights lit up the horizon as far as I could see.

THE END

To be alerted of new releases, please sign up for my mailing list here: http://eepurl.com/bghQb1

ABOUT THE AUTHOR

Boyd Craven III was born and raised in Michigan, an avid outdoors-man who has always loved to read and write from a young age. When he isn't working outside on the farm, or chasing a household of kids, he's sitting in his Lazy Boy, typing away.

http://www.boydcraven.com/

Facebook: https://www.facebook.com/boydcraven3

Email: boyd3@live.com

You can find the rest of Boyd's books on Amazon:
www.amazon.com/-/e/B00BANIQLG

Made in the USA
Middletown, DE
05 July 2019